The Place

Beyond the Dust Bowl

Author's note:

As a schoolteacher, it seems to me that the emphasis today is to recognize the differences and similarities in children. These variances from the "norm" are known as exceptionalities.

A migrant child's life unquestionably has a unique set of circumstances with which he or she must cope. Migrant life is by nature hard and dismal and cannot be truly appreciated unless experienced.

All of us have the ability to achieve career satisfaction, no matter our backgrounds. If each one of us gives back even a little of life's lessons, solicited or not, in an effort to teach, we too will learn along the way.

In this game of life, we all give and take, but we must always remember to be humble.

The Place
Beyond the Dust Bowl

By Ron Hughart

*" I wanted to have
friends sleep over so I
could show off our new
flush toilet. For me, this
was a real step forward
to the good life."*

Bear State Books
Exeter, California

Printed in the United States of America

Bear State Books

Post Office Box 96
Exeter, California 93221
(559) 592-6760
(559) 592-5779 fax
k1718@earthlink.net

ISBN: 1-892622-16-5

Hughart, Ron. 1949-

California History

First Printing, 2002

Dedicated to:

Chad, his wife Stacey, and our daughters Jodi, and Wendy.

My children are a testimony to my wife's and my abilities to separate right from wrong, good from evil, and to teach life's subtle differences. They have made us proud and hopefully we have given them a place to belong.

Love, Dad

Contents

1   "25" and "25"   1

2   The Repossession   7

3   The Retarded Boy   19

4   Summer Socks   35

5   Valley of Hunger   47

6   The Corral Fence   81

7   Tobacco Juice   87

8   Cricket   97

9   The Harley   103

10   Darrell   107

11   "Tailor-made"   127

12   The Badger   131

13   The Foreclosure   137

14   The Warden   143

15   The Move North   161

16   Olive Green   177

17   Exceptionality or Disability?   209

18   The First Day of School--Again   217

1   "25 and "25" (Continued)   223

ACKNOWLEDGMENTS

As a child, I was blessed to know four men other than family, who were significant in my life in a positive way right when I needed it most. They were; an old hermit named Irvy, two cowboys named Jim and Darrell and my eighth grade teacher, Mr. Light. To thank them, is to pass on their kindness to others as I've tried to do all of my life.

I'm very grateful for Larry Ronk's eloquent words about the author that so artfully captured the image of me shown on the back cover.

Chris Brewer, his wife Sally, and Jeff Burdick, most especially deserve special thanks for their guidance and editorial comments. I couldn't have finished this book without their knowledge and kindness.

A special thanks to others who read my manuscript and were supportive throughout this process. They are: Beth, Bill and Lorna, Carol; Carri, Dan and Connie; Debbie, Glenn and Jennie; Hank and Helen; Hope, Jeanette, Jeannie, Joy, Larry and Sheila; Laura, Leslie, Michelle, and Pam; Pete, Ola Mae, and Kelly; Sharon, Sandy, Tammy, and Teresa; and Rich and Sheila. Their thoughts and criticisms turned out to be my most valuable writing tool.

Finally, my family the most supportive of all, who have my love forever. Many, many, thanks to you all.

INTRODUCTION

After having been stripped from their simple, but stable childhoods growing up on farms in Oklahoma, Mom and Dad became lost "Okies" in the fruit and vegetable fields of California. As young married adults, but still in their teens, and not having any particular job skills other than working with their hands, they were forced into a migrant lifestyle to provide food for their starving family.

Mom and Dad had four children, Ronnie, Peggy, Steve and Sandy before either of them turned twenty-two. After a five-year gap, Billie Sue came along.

My folks were proud people and unwilling to accept handouts or any type of public assistance. Their dream was simple: to find forty acres of land to graze a few milk cows, grow a garden and raise their five children. Having farm animals; a horse to ride, cows for fresh milk, and chickens for eggs, was also important in living a good life.

Growing up I learned reality is harsh, and its onset should be accompanied with much explanation and caution. My parents, stifled by the harshness of their own reality as were so many around them, were more concerned about daily survival than the assimilation of their children into a social system, with which they themselves were unfamiliar.

Guidance, be it social, psychological, or behavioral, for the kids around the labor camps, was mostly delegated to the schools. Moving from camp to camp offered a myriad of translations of social rights and wrongs, unlocking a door to an uncontrolled environment where a child could become socially disoriented if not completely lost.

More often than not, I found myself searching deep inside my mind for some sort of rational reasoning to so many questions. I desperately wanted my world to make sense, so I tried to think through the trials and tribulations of my past and to help answer that which was now puzzling me. This self-imposed survival mode produced enough motivation to move forward into an uncertain future and exist in a world that thought of me as a "retard."

Even though I was misdiagnosed by my second grade teacher, the following years of residual ramification of having been told I was retarded, along with the hardships of being a family member of poor migrants, left me vulnerable at times and struggling for answers. This took much effort and I fought from one success or failure to the next.

Adults that leave positive impressions with children are blessings to us all. Parents are the most giving and forgiving adults in our lives. They are the people that we can depend on, and should not be less loved because of the tremendous changes occurring within us.

Some adults are angels that cross our paths at just the right time, and provide positive influences in our lives. Those individuals are the core reason for our self worth. For me, angels other than family members, numbered less than the total digits on one of my hands. They were my mom's father's best friend, Irvy, my eighth grade teacher, Mr. Light, and two cowboys named Jim and Darrell.

While sitting alone, at my backyard patio table after my fiftieth birthday party, a couple of candles reminded me of my childhood. Too busy being an adult, I had not thought of my earlier years in a long while.

Thinking back, my first thoughts began around the time two men came to our house and took our car away. This action sparked anger inside me, and hence the onset of my childhood memories. I was five years old and we lived in a little house on a hillside in Springville, California. Until then, I was impervious to much of life's difficulties.

The Place
Beyond the Dust Bowl

1

"25" and "25"

September 22, 1999, I opened the back door leading out to the patio area and heard many voices bursting forth in song. This was my fiftieth birthday. I'd barbequed for a few friends, but there was enough chicken to feed an army before being sent out on an errand to Visalia. The larger gathering wasn't really a surprise, but loads of fun. Everyone at the party wanted to pat me on the shoulder or shake my hand while making jokes about waiting dinner for me with a mouthful of food. Mixing this with a few hugs from the ladies; I smiled from one thank you to the next.

The urge to revel in every moment dominated my awareness. Time, as a spatial presence was almost chewable. I could hardly refrain from singing happy birthday to myself. Something about turning fifty made me want to cherish every moment.

The cake, a German Chocolate and my favorite, was adorned with four, three-inch white with red trimmed paraffin candles. This was done at my request, because a friend had recently told me I wasn't turning a half-century-old, but rather twice twenty-five. Instead of "50", the candles read "25" and "25."

I looked around at the smiling faces, then down at the flickering plumes of yellow and orange. I made the traditional birthday wish and blew out the flames.

The evening was a comfortable seventy-eight degrees; perfect for wearing shorts. It often rained on my birthday, but this night was great. A slight breeze carried whiffs of mild perfumes from the ladies, only to be trounced on by heavy smells of after-shave cascading from the men. The aroma of coffee began winding its way through the air mixing with other after dinner smells of cigars and cognac.

I sat down at the glass patio table just as a piece of birthday cake was being served to me. Harley Davidson paraphernalia came at me from every direction, a Harley T-shirt, a Harley calendar and mug, along with a mountain of Harley cards. Each card told of ancient artifacts that translated into AARP jokes or how mid-life crises might somehow be apropos for those of my advanced age. The 1994 Harley, a Heritage Softail I'd given myself only days before the party, served to qualify the verbal jesting now liberally filling the atmosphere. I had started my "scooter" three times for my guests, announcing to the world that I'd come of age.

I looked up at the grapes, Crimson Reds, hanging from my arbor and the white Christmas lights I'd strung throughout the vines. I leaned back in my chair in an attempt to hear my twenty-three year old son, Chad, asking folks to lift their glasses to the person he most admired. A lump grew in my throat, and some cigar smoking fool out by the pool began yelling, "Speech! Speech!"

The backyard was mostly bricked with cool decking surrounding a pond of lighted water, nice enough, but not at all conducive to greenery. Month's prior, desperate to grow something, I'd built a dozen vertical planter boxes covering the face of the detached garage wall. Shaded by the arbor, each planter box contained one or two of my favorite herbs. Fortunately, I leaned into a bristly sage and pretended it bothered me as I cleared my throat and somewhat composed myself. My son's toast had caught me totally off guard. I stood and told everyone I had no intention of writing thank you notes like girls do, but wanted to take this opportunity to be gracious and thank them personally for supporting me in my time of need. Chuckling surrounding me, and a faint "At least he's honest" came from someone inside the group. A voice leaped out, "To Ronnie!" Another voice, "Here, hear!" and everyone lifted his or her glass to me for the second time.

Refocusing on my cake, I noticed one set of the waxy "twenty-fives" had been pulled off the cake and was lying atop the glass table. The sight of these candles briefly sent my mind into a cavern of memories I'd not thought about for many years.

The second two candles still perched tall and statue-like in the waves of coconut and chocolate. With their foundation steadily decreasing in size, they were waiting their turn to be retired. The disappearing cake seemed to symbolize how fast time chips away at our stay here on earth, which made me all the more reminiscent.

The second pair of candles also represented most of my working career and the beginning of a third segment of my life, that hopefully would bring a healthy retirement, grandkids, and travel.

Folks visited for a time and eventually said their farewells, wishing me a happy birthday over and over again as they picked their way through the dining room, across the living room and out the front door.

"Great party Ron," Larry my postman friend chimed, last to leave, escorting his little family out the new antique screen door and following several other guests bidding each other a joyful goodnight.

"Thanks Larry, stay well, hope to see you soon," I replied in my most appreciative voice, while listening for the squeak I'd built into the screen door as it slowly shut toward me.

Earlier while inside the house, thanking everyone for coming, my thoughts lingered about what the first set of candles conjured up in my mind's eye. Now that the guests were gone, I felt a need to revisit my younger years. It suddenly occurred to me that hanging on to memories required a certain amount of revisiting, and I'd been lax these past few years.

I returned to the patio table, now cluttered with half-empty wineglasses, cigar butts, and left over smooshed cake in paper plates, each containing a red plastic fork with gummed up tines. I sat in the quiet still of the moment and noticed my cake supporting the second set of scorched candles. I plucked first the number "2" and then the number "5." I laid them down beside the fancy plate next to their twins denoting an official end to this segment of my life.

I noticed a clear glass candy dish shaped like an apple containing M&M's. I looked at the first set of candles signifying the first "tri-segment" of my life. Leaning forward, I reached out and grabbed a hand full of the multicolored candy morsels. I sat back in my chair under the calm of the arbor lights, and allowed my mind to drift. I saw myself as a child standing on the front porch of our tiny house located in the oak-infested foothills of Springville, California. I was holding some candies Mom bought because it was new on the store shelves this year. As I stared into my hand at the chocolate pea shaped tidbits, I wondered how those two tiny "M's" had been painted on each peace.

2

The Repossession

Our house was small; it had no back door, because the back half was sunken into the hillside. I was five years old turning six in three weeks, and I loved to run from the rocky hillside out onto our grassy roof to play.

I had no idea how long we'd lived there. Memories, prior to that summer before starting school, were sketchy at best. I liked the Hobbit-like house and the creek out front that had crawdads in it.

I also liked my pony. Dad had traded a saddle for a small black Shetland pony I named Blackie. We kept him staked out on a rope to graze the hillside and moved him often to fresh grass. On one occasion Blackie ate his fill on our roof.

~.~.~

My mom, Doris, was always thin and had naturally curly, almost kinky, brown hair. She probably had the hardest life of any of us. She had polio as a child and it left her with a lower lip that drooped. She had to get false teeth, having lost her permanent teeth at an early age, probably due to malnutrition.

Dad was the most handsome man I ever saw. His grandmother on his mom's side was full-blooded Cherokee and it showed in Dad. He had the typical Indian high cheekbones and coal black hair. He was defiantly the strong silent type.

I was the eldest of four kids born about a year apart. I had two sisters and a brother. In chronological order was my sister Peggy, who liked books; my brother Steven, who liked playing with Peggy's dolls; and Sandy, who enjoyed sitting on Dad's saddle he kept on the floor in a corner of the living room.

To me, the other children in our house were just younger people who made lots of noise and got in the way much of the time.

Once in awhile, my grandpa, John D., my mom's dad, who lived nearby came over for dinner and brought his fiddle to play out on the front porch after the evening meal. He lived with his young son Jimmy. I didn't know Jimmy very well because he was thirteen and always swimming at the river with his friends. Grandpa's wife, Jewel, had died of cancer about the time I was born. I wasn't close to Grandpa because he seemed preoccupied and kept to himself a lot. He carried little weight on his small-framed body. He wasn't in good health, constantly in and out of the TB hospital located just on the other side of the same hill where we lived. Grandpa's breath often smelled of wine and a glass of the libation was never far from his reach.

Grandpa had a best friend named Irvy. Irvy was an old hermit prospector that lived in a one-room log cabin in the foothills about eight miles east of our house. He mined for gold and crystals and came to town about once a month for supplies and to have a glass of wine with Grandpa.

Irvy was on the short side, but a little bigger than Grandpa. Dad said although Irvy was lean, he was also a tough old guy and a hard worker. He wore a white beard and round spectacles as he called them, sometimes perched about half way down the bridge of his nose. He wore a brown, floppy hat that was always cocked back on his head, which he never took off. Irvy had one normal leg and the other was made of wood below the knee. He told me he'd lost his right leg at the age of twelve from complications after an accident while chopping wood.

When Grandpa came to dinner he'd usually bring Irvy when his hermit friend was in town. Irvy liked Spam sandwiches and brought several cans of the preserved meat each time he visited around suppertime.

Mom opened the cans of Spam and sliced the meat into sandwich-sized pieces. She'd build sandwiches by cutting up an onion to go with the meat and spreading mayonnaise between a couple slices of Langendorf bread. I dearly loved the taste of Spam, onion, and mayonnaise together on white bread. I tasted the special sandwiches in my mouth at the mere sight of Grandpa and Irvy walking up the hill toward our house.

Irvy didn't seem to like talking with adults, except Grandpa of course, but enjoyed telling stories to us kids.

Irvy shared many things with me. Once he told me he shaved off his beard and went blind until it grew back. He also said I should wear a beard when I grew up so I'd see things more clearly. He laughed and I thought it great fun to listen to his tall tales.

I was completely enthralled with Irvy's wooden leg and was constantly asking him questions about it. Irvy told me he whittled out his own peg leg when he needed one. He said he'd dig up a willow tree root and cut it just above where it widened into the trunk of the tree. Then he hollowed out the wide part of the root to just the right depth to insert the stub of his leg. Finally, he cut the pointy end to whatever length enabled him to stand level. Irvy said he'd take rubber tire tubing and line the hollowed out part for comfort, then fasten a length of tubing to the outside of the willow branch leg threading it up and through his belt. He'd bring the strip of rubber back down to the inside of the peg leg where he again attached it with nails. This not only held Irvy's leg in place, but also allowed him to bend his knee without the fake leg falling off. I was told Irvy had a wooden leg and foot he could put a shoe on that was called his "Sunday go to meet'n leg" but I never saw it.

One autumn evening after supper, Grandpa was playing his fiddle on the front porch while Irvy danced a jig, which he often did. A car with two men pulled up into our driveway. The passenger, a man with yellow hair, slid out of his car away from the driver and unfolded right up toward the sky. He raked dirty fingers across his forehead, and the red streaks looked angry and mean. He nodded and pretended to be polite, but he scared me. The round-faced driver, pulling himself out of the car with one hand, while grabbing at a half-smoked cigar with the other and semi-rolled out of the driver's side of his vehicle. His heavy beard collected dirt and sweat in the fat rings of his neck. As he stood, his head covered with a dirty bent straw hat, didn't reach the shoulders of his partner.

The short chubby guy took off his hat, exposing his thick matted gray hair, looked over in the direction of Mom and said, "Evening, ma'am."

Then the same man looked over at my dad and said, "Sorry sir, but I have to take your car. Can I please have the key?"

My dad didn't say a word. His eyes showed me his pain. Even at such a young age, I knew that Dad needed our car to drive to work. He reached into his left pocket, pulled out a single silver key and tossed it to the man. The plump red-faced fellow started to say something else but stopped short and said, "Thanks, man." He backed down the hill a few feet, turned, got into our car and drove it away, followed closely by the blond headed man now driving the stumpy man's car.

Mom was crying and Dad went inside the house. I wanted to run after the cars and throw rocks at the bad men for making my mom and dad so sad; my fear had turned to anger.

Irvy must have noticed my frustration. As Grandpa began to play a slow tune, Irvy, with a serious look on his face, put his hand on my shoulder and guided me to the porch steps where we sat down.

"Look over there to the evening sky and notice the red in the autumn twilight" he said as he pointed. "It's beautiful. Sometimes it looks different, but it's always beautiful. Remember, there will be many more evenings that will come after good things happen than there are evenings like this one. Ronnie, you might be too young to understand this, but I'm going to tell you anyway.

You've just experienced something sad that upset your mom and dad a great deal. Don't let this one bad thing upset you. It's important to know that each day is special and if you worry too much, time will pass quickly, but if you enjoy today, time will seem to pass more slowly. If you slow down and allow yourself to be who you are, your thoughts will be more interesting and special. In turn, you'll become more special and interesting to others around you. Ronnie, a better life is yours for the taking."

I looked up into Irvy's eyes and he said, "It's okay if you don't fully understand right now. Just remember to look ahead and know that life is good. Feel the goodness in nature and be honest to yourself when thinking about other people. There are reasons for everything. Just like tonight when those men came to get your car. Those weren't bad men here tonight, they were a couple of gentleman paid to repossess your dad's car because he couldn't keep up the payments on it. Your dad will get another car and who knows, it will probably be better than the one taken away. Your father is not mad at those guys for taking your car. He is upset with himself for not having the money to keep them from taking the car." Your parents will be okay, it's just a little set back they'll get through. It's okay to be sad for your parents, but don't be mad at those two men just because your folks are unhappy. Everything will work out and there will be more good days than bad ones."

Irvy was the first adult in my life that showed me how to lay the foundation for reasoning. His many thematic stories, all having morals to them, showed me the importance of understanding differences in people, and how I might apply those differences to my life in a positive way.

Irvy was a hermit prospector and my friend. The photograph was taken in the early sixties by Charles Rich, founder of SCICON. Rick Mitchell, Director of the Clemmie Gill School of Science and Conservation (SCICON), supplied the photo.

It was cool the next morning as I stood in the doorway and watched Dad walk down the grassy drive, carrying his dented black metal lunch pail. Steam rose from the hot cup of coffee he sipped on as he disappeared from my sight.

He worked at a sawmill about four miles up the road north of town and it saddened me to watch him walk to work.

I felt bad about our car being taken away and wondered how long Dad would stay sad. I played out front near the creek all day, so I'd be sure to be there the minute Dad returned. I wanted to see his eyes, which were my only source of information as to how this stoic man felt.

Dad did return and that evening Mom and Dad spent a lot of time talking to each other. My folks didn't seem so sad and that made me feel a lot better inside.

I was excited about the upbeat mood around the house. Grandpa and Irvy were bringing Spam again on Saturday and Dad usually watched me ride my pony on Sundays. I thought about what Irvy had told me about more good days than bad ones.

~.~.~

"Ronnie! Take off your clothes, I have to wash them out for school tomorrow," Mom shouted.

I was running Blackie up the driveway and fell off upon receiving this news of school. It was Sunday so Dad was home from work. He walked over, seeing I was about to cry said, "Don't cry. Mom will make us sell your pony."

School! I thought. What was school? I knew the word, but the idea of me ever going to school really never crossed my mind. I was stunned and got sick to my stomach. Clutching my right arm, I walked over and fed the crayfish by throwing up in the creek.

The next morning, I got up and tried to eat some mush, but I was too nervous. Mom walked me to school. The creek in front of our house ran along side the east fence of the schoolyard, so it wasn't very far to have to travel.

The school was full of adults and children. I didn't see anyone who looked remotely familiar. We went into a large hallway and through a door with lots of glass in it. There were gold and black letters on the glass part, but I didn't know what they meant. I stood beside Mom at a yellowish counter taller than me. Mom was busy writing down something as I looked around at the walls covered with different sizes and colors of paper with lots of writing on them. The smell of this place was strange to me. It smelled like the inside of our old car mixed with the sweetness of cherry Kool-Aid.

Mom finished writing and left me with a woman wearing dark pointy glasses and a large, green, sack dress with a gold flower on the front of it. The lady told me she was going to be my first grade teacher and took me by the hand, which still hurt from the fall off my pony, to a room somewhere inside the huge brick building. She opened a door and pointed to a desk inside.

"That one will be yours, Mr. Ronnie," she said.

As I walked to my desk, several other kids who all seemed to know each other began filling the room. Everyone was talking and laughing, except during the time they were gawking at me. The teacher stood by her desk in front of the room and pointed to some words on the blackboard behind her. She said the words read, "Mrs. Webb." She talked for a very long time, and finally told the class to take out their pencils as she passed out sheets of paper to the class. The pencils were dark green and about two or three times wider than any pencil I had ever held before.

I had to pee and didn't know what to do. I had to go so badly, I was afraid to move. I didn't know if I had to ask to go, or if I could just leave. Even if I left, I didn't know where to find a bathroom. I thought about walking home at one point, but too late. The pee just came out! I strained to stop, but it was no use. I sat there in wet pants and noticed a puddle forming on the floor between my feet. I was hoping that no one else noticed my predicament. Just then I heard the teacher tell the class to go out to recess.

She walked over to me and said, "Come with me Ronnie, your mother is waiting outside."

I wondered if Mom had been waiting outside the classroom all morning.

"Here he is Mrs. Hughart, I'm sorry," my teacher said.

"I'll take him home to change and bring him back after lunch," Mom said back to my teacher as she grabbed my hurt hand.

We went home and I took off my pants. Mom hung them on the clothesline to dry in the sun. As I'd never worn underwear, I waited wrapped up in a bed sheet to hide my nakedness. Mom had to dry this pair of pants because they were the only pair I owned at the time. Finally the pants dried and Mom took me back to school.

It was now lunch recess, so I went out to the playground and stood at the corner of the brick building.

A girl that I recognized from my class because of the dark pink dress she was wearing, walked up to me and said, "You peed in your pants didn't you?"

"No!" I shouted, "Go away!" It was not a good day for me. I was mortified, smelled of pee, and my right arm was killing me it hurt so bad. A blue green ring now encircled my right wrist, which was swollen to the point I had trouble moving it. I kept my injury covered beneath my long sleeve shirt because Mom would make me sell my pony if she saw my bruised wrist. The bell rang, and even though I didn't want to follow Miss "Pinky Stinky" back to my classroom, the dark pink dress proved to be a beacon and only navigational tool available for me to find my way back.

When I got back to the classroom, I pretended to be writing and drew pictures of myself sitting in a corner, without friends and all alone. I fought hard to hold back the tears.

A few weeks later we sold Blackie and bought another old car. We moved three or four times over the next two years, eventually living in a run down two story house in the middle of a cotton field near a place called Stone Corral and still in California. Not yet finished with my second year of school, I had already attended four schools in my short career.

3

The Retarded Boy

It was hot on that old, faded, yellow school bus, riding home for the last time that summer. Today was the last day of my second grade year. I looked at my feet dangling from the dingy, green Naugahyde seat, and I didn't notice the cracks beside me caused by the hot sun shining down through the tinted windows.

"Ronnie! Do you want off here, or are you going back to school with me?"

I'd been a hundred miles away. I was trying to figure out why my classmates had a "three" marked on their report cards, and mine was marked "two." I was fairly certain I'd flunked, but no one had said anything to me.

I just knew it had something to do with my teacher telling Mom I was retarded.

I'd only been going to this school for three weeks, but had already made an impression on my teacher. I was retarded, she'd told my parents, and I wondered if it was true. My report card from my previous school made mention of my poor health, but my grades seemed okay.

TEACHER'S Comments	PARENT'S Comments
FIRST QTR. Better work habits would help his work — But he has improved a lot.	*Mrs. Hughart* Parent's Signature
SECOND QTR. Ronnie was getting along so fine. But hasn't been feeling so well the last few weeks. Hope his cold etc get over soon.	*Mrs. Hughart* Parent's Signature
THIRD QTR. I really feel that Ronnie's work will improve more when his health is up to par!	*Mrs. Hughart* Parent's Signature
FOURTH QTR. Its been a joy to have Ronnie. We hope his health improves for next year	*Mrs. Hughart* Parent's Signature

Ronnie's second grade report card that makes mention of his failing health.

20

As I jumped off the seat, I cut my hand on a jagged piece of hard plastic. Bleeding, hot, and a little confused, I got off the bus.

Dust mixed with diesel smoke choked me. I thought the driver was mad as the bus roared away.

~.~.~

We followed the fruit--sort of. My dad sometimes stayed on after the harvest to drive tractor or irrigate. Sometimes he milked cows. We weren't like some migrant families, moving in a pattern or following a particular fruit. We just moved.

I was eight now. My siblings often depended on me to help them. Sometimes I'd help Mom by straightening the part in my brother's hair before school and I even French braided my sisters' hair from time to time. Sometimes I'd cook oatmeal and feed everyone. I took on this parental role out of necessity to relieve my already over burdened parents.

Mom didn't work outside the house. She loved country western music and reading romance novels. She quit school in the seventh grade to help her family work in the fields. Mom worried endlessly about not having enough money to buy ample groceries between paychecks.

She enjoyed playing cards, particularly Rummy. Mom often sought out neighbor ladies to play cards. There were many other women in the "same boat" as Mom; Living in labor camps, scrimping from week to week with too many mouths to feed; staying home all day putting used jigsaw puzzles together, only to find two of the pieces were missing upon completing the puzzle.

Mom seemed happiest when she met up with other ladies near by to play cards with, and perhaps share a cold Pepsi Cola.

My dad, a cowboy at heart, took most any job to feed us kids. He liked having a horse. If we got a horse, we usually had to sell it when we moved. Not having a horse trailer and often not knowing where we were going meant leaving Dad's recreation behind. His life's desire was to become a world champion cowboy. He often spoke about his favorite job, which had been breaking horses to ride at the Tulare County Fair Grounds. Dad often told me about climbing aboard a young colt and riding it until the "buck" was gone. I marveled at his toughness and delighted in his stories because I could see it made him happy.

I learned a lot about horses from my dad. By the age of nine, I was putting shoes on our horse. Dad taught me how deep to cut the horses' hooves with sharp trimming pliers and to rasp them down to a smooth surface. He showed me how to store horseshoe nails in the cuff of my Levis, so they'd be readily accessible while nailing on the horseshoes.

Though Dad was not an educated man, he had a lot of knowledge about horses, which I admired greatly. He too had quit school early after only one year of high school. He didn't read or write very well, destined to a lifetime of labor in the fields.

Working in the fields, whether harvesting whatever fruit was in season, or ripe, and ready to pick, or plowing the fields, left Dad exhausted much of the time.

Mom and Dad spent a great deal of time remembering the past and hoping the future would bring good fortune. Much of each evening was spent talking about what once was and very little discussion about the days' events. The topic of school was rarely mentioned except for an occasional, "What did you learn in school today?" Knowing school was not a subject meaningful to our parents, the answer was invariably "Nutin." This answer stopped the conversation cold and allowed everyone to go on to more important topics, like which fruit was in season next month and how to save enough money to get to wherever it was growing.

Both my parents grew up in Oklahoma. As children they lived within fifty miles of each other, Mom in Haskell County and Dad to the south in Laflore County. Neither knew the other until they met in Pixley, California, after their families migrated in hopes of finding a better life for themselves.

~.~.~

The Great Drought and Depression forced Mom's parents off their land in the late 1930's and westward to find work.

My dad's mother, Nancy, had not heard from her husband Leonard, Len as everyone called him, in over a year during World War II, and decided to move to California to find work. In the mid 1940's Grandma spent weeks selling all their possessions and the family farm. She took her three sons, my dad David Lee, my

Uncle Pete, Leonard Hudson Jr., and my Uncle Ed, Edward Lee, to the bus station. As she was waiting to board, her husband, my Grandpa, who had been a gunner on a naval battle ship, stepped off the very same bus, home from the war. This began my grandparents' trek westward.

Grandma and Grandpa bought a small house in Tulare but it soon burned, leaving Dad's family, literally, with nothing but the clothes on their backs, and forcing them to live in a tent near Pixley, California.

During the time my grandparents lived in Tulare, Dad attended high school there where he knew Bob Mathias, the Olympian. He seemed very proud to have known Mr. Mathias and would often speak of him.

~.~.~

That night, the last day of my second grade year, was bad. After Dad got home from driving a Caterpillar all day making irrigation ditches, Mom told him I was going to have to repeat the second grade. Dad walked over to the small sink and took off his hat and shirt. I knew he'd have no verbal reaction, but I dreaded to see the disappointment in his eyes. He slid his shirt to the floor near the back door moving slowly so his movement wouldn't fill the air with dust. His skin shone pasty and wet with sweat where the sun never touched. His red, watery eyes sat deep in his face, and his skin was caked with chalk like dirt.

He took a long time to wash. The dirt and sweat had built up thick layers of crust on his face and arms. Dad walked across the tiny room holding a small blue hand towel. He'd mostly dried himself by the time he reached the dining table. As he sat down, I noticed the chair was made of the same kind of plastic as the seat in the school bus. The chair, too, had cracks in it! I hoped no one would cut his or her hand as I had earlier. He sat down to dinner. There was one egg in our house, which Mom was frying up for Dad's supper.

Just as Mom was putting the egg, cooked hard so there wouldn't be any waste, on the plate in front of Dad, my little brother, Steve, came into the room and told Dad he was still hungry. Our dinner had consisted of mayonnaise and onions. I'd quartered an onion and pulled off one section at a time, using it to scoop the mayonnaise.

My father, hearing Steve, simply pushed away from the table and the plate containing the only sustenance in our house and went directly to bed.

~.~.~

A few days later, we all loaded up in our old green Hudson and headed out to Arizona.

We always left furniture behind when we moved. Generally we left stuff that we couldn't tie down somewhere on the car.

When we got to where we were going, it was easier to locate a second-hand store and buy more furniture. We never left important stuff though, like guns, saddles and clothes. We always had three or four cardboard boxes full of stuff we'd gotten free from different kinds of grocery supplies.

Mom bought specially marked oatmeal to get a free spoon or fork inside. She also bought large laundry soapboxes containing towels, and sometimes the measuring cup doubled as a teacup. All of our silverware and dishes came from some sort of food box. My sister Peggy rejoiced to get snap-beads in tubs of margarine.

~.~.~

I took my tricycle out to get loaded up, because to me it was important stuff.

Everyone was ready--Mom, Dad, my oldest sister Peggy, Steve, and the little one, Sandy. They were all excited to begin another adventure and to see a new state.

~.~.~

We were always going to find ourselves a "place" and this was no exception. The "place" would be a house and a barn, somewhere near a creek with good fishing. Of course, if you had a place, you'd have a horse to ride, a cow to milk, chickens to tend, and a garden to grow things that Mom could put into jars for later use. To Mom and Dad, a "place" was happiness and contentment, which no longer existed in their lives. By now, I recognized the desperation in my parents to somehow regain the joy and security that owning property once afforded them.

Looking up, I saw my tricycle on its side and under the edge of the front porch. I yelled out, "My trike, my trike!"

Dad, already backing out and looking over his shoulder, uttered in a half breath, "You're eight. Too old for a trike."

Ronnie riding his tricycle that was left behind when leaving for Arizona.

The next four days were the worst four days of my life. We had virtually no food, no real place to lie down and sleep, and our drinking water hung in a canvas bag tied to the front grill of the Hudson, which wasn't really green, because the sun had faded it to nearly a gray color.

It was damned hot! Six people had to somehow sleep, eat and sometimes go to the bathroom in that hot musty smelling, dilapidated automobile. One dark night I had to pee, so I picked up an empty pop bottle, got down on my knees in the floorboard behind the front seat, and began taking care of business. I must have drunk a lot of the hot water that day, because I couldn't stop! With only one pop bottle available, I was horrified when I peed all over my hands, my little brother's shoes, and flooded the floorboard.

Old gray Hudson parked at a "filling station" somewhere on the road in Arizona in 1957.

During the day we drove from one ranch or farm to another. We stopped; Dad went to see if he could work there for money, and if it was all right for us to live there. We had to stop under some shade during the middle of the day and drive around only in the early morning and evenings, so our car would quit overheating. We drove, stopped, drove, overheated, stopped, and then drove some more.

I woke up the first morning with a severe earache. My ear hurt so badly, I remember having trouble focusing my eyes and my skin on the side of my face was numb to the touch. We drove for hours and Mom said something to Dad. A little while later, Dad pulled over under a shade tree and stopped the car. He took out a cigarette and put an exploding match to the end of it. I remember Dad's face being unusually sad. His eyes were shut, shielding themselves from the cloud of sulfur drifting up from the blackened match, and his shoulders slumped forward, in an attempt to catch a quick respite. He told me to crawl up front with him and Mom. Dad took a huge drag off the cigarette and blew the smoke into my left ear. After repeating this several times, Mom told me the warm smoke would help my ear to stop hurting.

No one really knew if the home remedies really worked. Mom would sometimes put a teaspoon of whisky in the baby's bottle of milk to cure an upset stomach. I often wondered if the whisky really helped or if the booze made the baby drunk and the natural reaction was to fall asleep. With no money to go to the doctor, there wasn't much else to do.

I pretended the smoke helped, so my parents wouldn't worry so much. My ear kept hurting for another day and gradually subsided on its own.

Though my ear quit hurting, I still felt bad. I was becoming weaker and weaker. I wasn't eating much of anything, and I was so skinny by now every protruding rib told its story of a losing battle to stay healthy.

Four days later and totally exhausted, we pulled into Grandma's driveway where we had started this trip and others so many times before. Mom and Dad drove until we had just enough money and gas to return to

Grandma's. I thought of it as the "point of no return" like an airplane pilot reaches and is forced to return to home base. Grandma's was the "hub" of our adventures, our "home base" or sanctuary for a time out to regroup before moving on to whatever it was we were looking for.

We had spent two whole days in Arizona before reaching our "point of no return". Two days I wouldn't care to repeat.

Dad's parents lived with his sixteen years old brother, Ed, in Farmersville, a small farming community centrally located in California's San Joaquin Valley. Grandma's was a place where my family went to heal. We could clean up, sometimes eat fried chicken and watch television. After a day or so Dad would drive off by himself, find a job somewhere, come back for us, and all was well for a few weeks or months.

My grandparents never said anything about our excursions, because I knew they understood what we were looking for and were supportive of our efforts. They had once owned a place back home in Oklahoma. It was forty acres with a house and a barn near a creek that had lots of fish in it. There were chickens to tend, a cow to milk, a horse to ride, and even a swimming hole with snakes in it. They had milk to drink everyday, eggs to eat everyday, and they could eat something from a canning jar everyday if they wanted. Stories about "The Place" back home were often revisited while staying at Grandma's.

It was decided that because of my languishing state, my parents were going to leave me with my grandparents in Farmersville to heal for the summer.

Dad left for the day and got a job. Upon his return he told us that he'd gotten a job milking cows and we could drink all the cold fresh milk we could hold. Grandma cooked fried chicken for super that evening in celebration of our good fortune.

Mom and Dad left the next morning to where Dad had found work. I wanted to go with them, but was glad to be able to sleep on a mattress for a while. I told myself that I'd only be at Grandma's for a week or so and then go home after I rested up.

Two more days passed and I was having trouble sitting up. The trip to Arizona had taken its toll on me. At the end of the second day, I still hadn't gotten out of bed.

The next morning my grandmother took me to see a doctor. By this time, I needed help to stand and walk. Grandma called my Aunt Reba to assist me. When we got into the car, I didn't have enough strength to hold my head up, so Aunt Reba held my head in her lap. It was the weekend, so we went to the doctor's house in the country near Lemoncove, a tiny foothill community a short distance from where the Doctor's office was located in Exeter.

Dr. Buckman was small in stature, but big inside. He was a kind man and made me feel safe and warm inside. He asked if I hurt anywhere. My sides always hurt when I was hungry from pushing in so hard, I guess.

I told Dr. Buckman nothing hurt. He swallowed and his face showed a hint of worry. My sides had quit hurting about a week before going to Grandma's house. I supposed my body was shutting down. After he examined me, Dr. Buckman told me I needed to drink lots of cod liver oil, and if I drank it with orange juice it wouldn't taste so bad.

Grandma told me later that Dr. Buckman said I soon would have had rickets, a disabling bone disease caused from a lack of vitamin D, and I'd been brought to him just in time to prevent other serious complications. He also told Grandma I had a slight wheezing in my chest, probably due to asthma. He said I'd more than likely grow out of it, but if I complained of not being able to get enough air to call him right away.

Dr. Buckman drove out to check up on me from his office in Exeter, a small town three miles east of Farmersville, where I'd always been told the rich people lived. He made sure I was eating enough and left a bottle of cod liver oil if needed. I later learned Dr. Buckman never charged for those house calls.

I felt bad when I thought about my brother and sisters, because I knew what they had to eat or better yet, didn't have to eat. I was especially sad when Grandma fixed fried chicken. Guilt got the best of me and I'd always asked Grandpa to take me home. It didn't seem right that I was eating eggs every morning, and everyone else in my family having to eat mush.

~.~.~

The summer passed quickly, and I'd seen my family only twice during the last two months. Dad's job milking cows wasn't too far from where we last lived, but in a different school district. I was glad to be changing schools this time, because no one knew I was going to have to repeat the second grade. I figured if I didn't tell anyone, no one would be the wiser, and if I stayed quiet, perhaps I'd hide my retardation.

Moving back to cold floors to sleep on and eating mainly beans and potatoes was hard for me. I felt guilty for living the past few weeks in luxury eating fried chicken and going fishing with Grandpa. Uncle Ed took me riding on his new motor scooter and bought me ice cream and sodas. I wanted to tell Mom and Dad I liked living in one place where meals were regular and the bed was soft and warm. This thought caused me to be ashamed of myself. How could I have had such horrible thoughts?

I returned home and after about a week, word that Uncle Ed had been killed in a motor scooter accident sent me into a depression. He and a friend were going to the movies in Visalia and hit a train before leaving Farmersville killing them both.

This move would prove to be the beginning of my life's struggles with success and defeat. I was embarking on a journey of rights and wrongs and a catalogue of mistakes that would mold me into the person I am today.

Living with the excitement of hope and feeling the very real pain of hopelessness, I began a trek of where the realization of assimilation and life's lessons started for me. I withdrew from those around me and lived within my thoughts.

4

Summer Socks

Five moves and four schools later, I was finishing up my fifth grade year. My family had recently moved back to the school district in Seville where I'd failed the second grade. I'd already been challenged by the school bully, but really didn't want the school year to end. I wanted to go to school because I got to eat a hot lunch every day. During the week I'd have to eat oatmeal or Cream of Wheat for breakfast. For dinner, we ate beans and potatoes, or potatoes and beans, take your pick. I didn't like going to a school that didn't serve lunch, because then I'd have to eat apple butter on biscuits or on "light bread," which is what we called white bread, for my midday meal.

On the first Saturday of the month when Dad got paid, the whole family went to the grocery store. We'd buy 100 pounds of potatoes, 50 pounds of Pinto beans, and a sack of flour. The flour sacks, which usually bore colorful flowers, turned into a sundress for one of my sisters about a month later. My brother and I never got any flour-sack shirts though, and I often wondered why. Perhaps it was the flowers. Each payday, usually Saturdays, Mom always bought a small jar of mayonnaise, a head of lettuce, a yellow onion, one tomato, a loaf of "light bread" and a pound of hamburger.

About once a month Mom bought a half-gallon of Neapolitan ice milk. It was called Neapolitan because it was stripped with one-third chocolate, one-third vanilla and one-third strawberry. We called it ice cream, but it was ice milk.

At one of the small grocery stores that we visited there was a large, bald man who worked behind the meat counter. Charlie was his name. He had a remnant of hair circling around to the back of his head, just above both his ears.

Charlie got to know me after a while. We had a game. If he could get the poundage on the hamburger right on the first attempt, I had to sweep his floor, but if he got it wrong, and he always got it wrong, he'd let me have a licorice whip that was as long as I was tall. My mother was anxious about it, not wanting charity and all, but Charlie just shrugged. "He's already a candidate for a Halloween skeleton, he's so thin. With all that growing he's doing, I mean. I don't mean any disrespect. Hard to keep these growing kids filled up, isn't it?" Charlie said clumsily.

It was not until much later that I figured out why Charlie always put too much meat on our order. I must have been a pitiful sight to behold.

~.~.~

We'd have fried hamburgers to eat, and Double Colas, or 10,2&4, (Dr. Pepper), to drink every Saturday night Dad got paid.

~.~.~

Well, I passed the fifth grade and no one seemed to remember I'd been retarded. That was the summer I decided not to go as hungry anymore, as I had in my youth. Even though I often helped in the fields, picking cotton and so on, I wanted a job of my own. There was an old beat up lawn mower where we lived, which had given me my entrepreneurial idea, so I fixed it up and got it running!

I mowed the neighbor lady's lawn for fifty cents a week. Nelly lived a quarter mile away, which was ten miles closer than the next nearest neighbor. Since I had to push the mower that really only had three wheels because the rubber was mostly off the left rear tire, I only mowed Nelly's lawn. She sometimes let me mow it twice a week. I began my working career that fateful summer and I've not stopped since. I was ten years old and the year was 1960. That summer yielded nine dollars and fifty cents, which I gave to my folks to help buy groceries.

~.~.~

September rolled around and I started yet another new school. I liked school except for the one boy who was at the top of the pecking order and existed in every school. On the second day there, two tall and thin seventh grade boys sneaked up and grabbed me from behind. Out of nowhere stood Mr. Top 'o the Butting Order, an eighth grader that out-weighed me by at least

100 pounds. He was tall, had dirty blond hair, and a horrible crop of white-headed pimples on his face. My frailness must have been an enticement causing an involuntary reaction in his type.

The brute said, "I hear yur parents 'er Okies. Guess that means yur born on a ditch-bank somers, don't it?"

Of course he was referring to a little question and answer session I had with my teacher the day before in front of the entire class. My teacher had asked where my parents were from, and I'd answered, "Oklahoma."

I knew I was going to take a beating, because I'd been in this situation many times before. So I said, "Yep, but that's better than not knowing who my father was, like you."

I was absolutely dead on with my prediction! His buddies pinned my arms and the beating began! I refused to yell out or cry and I think that impressed the goon squad. The King of the Hill kicked me one last time before the bell ending the recess rang.

I looked straight into his eyes and said, "Now, try me alone."

To everyone's surprise, including me, the two goons released their grip. Mr. Tough Guy showed an instant of shock, which was all I needed to see, because even though he was telling me what he was going to do to me the next time we met, I knew my beatings at this school were over. I didn't lay a hand on the bully, but I'd won the battle.

Sixth grade photo of Ronnie taken at the Stone Corral School in Seville about the time he was assaulted by the eight-grade bully and his goon squad.

I had much experience with bullies, even at such a young age. There were not as many bullies challenging me in the labor camps, but there were a few. Children at the labor camps had similar backgrounds and tended to stick together rather than fight each other, sometimes practicing on each other. This "play fighting" was sometimes beneficial in a one-on-one fight.

There were a few bullies who liked picking on my little brother, Steve. He seemed somewhat effeminate and refused physical confrontations. I had to fight many of his battles in the camps as well as those in school.

In one incident a couple of years earlier, a tough guy came over to our trailer and called my little brother out to fight. This boy was much bigger than Steve, the usual bully type, plus he was carrying a big stick in his hand. I went outside and confronted the bad guy. Steve was a first grader, and the staff-in-hand, want-to-be-Viking, was a third grader like me. I liked this guy's haircut. He had a Mohawk and I liked Mohawks. We probably could have been friends if he hadn't had such big chips on his shoulders. I remember his dad was real mean to him.

~.~.~

He lunged at me with the pole and I stepped inside his swing on the attack. I grabbed a bunch of flesh with my teeth at the base of his neck and bit down as hard as humanly possible. He pushed away, and as I looked up, I spit out a chunk of his skin and muscle hitting him in the face with it. He started to cry and ran away, never to bother us again, other than squinty seedy stares from afar once in a while. Dad gave both Steve and me Mohawk haircuts that night, which we wore for the rest of the summer. I felt sorry for the other boy in the court, because he was afraid of his dad and hated everyone else because of it; and I thought that very sad.

Sometimes even my sisters were challenged to fight, but not nearly as often as I was. Fighting was just a part of life. I didn't like it, but what could I do? I almost never told my parents about the many beatings, except of course for those times my lip was split or the evidence was as plain as the broken nose on my face. I think my nose was broken eleven times in elementary school alone. If Mom found out I'd been fighting she spanked me.

~.~.~

After only a week, my teacher stopped me in the hallway and handed me three pairs of boys' socks. He told me that he'd found them in the teachers' room, and no one knew where they'd come from. My teacher wasn't very good at what he was trying to do, but he was a good man for his efforts. I was just a little embarrassed; because I was wearing tennis shoes that had huge holes in them and of course, no socks.

I justified the awkwardness of the situation by thinking to myself that it was summertime, and socks weren't really necessary in the summertime.

In August of that same year, my parents were visiting with another family that was moving to Salinas, California. These folks were going to go to the Salinas Valley, work in the potato fields for three months, save up all their money and buy a "place" which of course appealed to my dad. These folks were also from Oklahoma. Stories of life back home raised everyone's spirits and kept us up well into the wee hours of the morning.

Dad had bought a boat just before our last move. He never put it in the water though, because Mom wouldn't let him. The previous owner had been killed in a boating accident and Mom thought it was jinxed. We used the boat as a trailer to haul our stuff. Dad liked the boat so much; he painted it red, white, and blue on two separate occasions. Having no top, it was easy enough to load up our stuff and head out to where ever the money was.

Off we went to greener pastures. I thought to myself, why the H-E-double "L" tooth picks not? What is the worst thing that could happen? We might wind up in another labor camp. No biggie. Perhaps we'd have to go back to Grandma's to heal? I liked watching her TV anyway! I secretly wished though, that we were going to pick apricots rather than potatoes.

~.~.~

I remembered our trip to Arizona and how we'd stop after dark to pick corn or watermelons to eat, you know, like Huck Finn did. There was one apricot tree in particular that was unforgettable. The fruit was incredibly delicious, and how I wished we could have a tree of our own or pick them for money.

Perhaps it was the location of the apricot tree that most attracted me. It was what I'd pictured in my mind's eye when my parents talked about their own childhoods. The tree was growing along side a creek that ran cool and clear. There were lots of other kinds of shade trees. I remember watching small tufts of white material floating in the air. Dad said that the almost hair like puffs were coming from cottonwood trees. The cottonwood trees lined the stream banks so thickly the whiffs of cotton-like stuff piled against the surrounding fauna resembling snow banks.

I enjoyed eating a ripe apricot, or cutting open a juicy watermelon, or roasting corn over the open flame of the campfire. In the evening, the breeze was cool against my clammy skin and a refreshing gift after splashing the creek water on my face.

Sometimes we'd go swimming with our clothes on. Mom gave us a bar of Ivory soap and told us to wash ourselves, including our clothes. Dad always said, "Might as well kill two birds with one stone." We only did this if there was enough time for our clothes to air-dry before dark, because they were often the only clothes we had if we were on the road and between jobs.

After dark, Mom and Dad told us kids stories about their own childhood and how they'd go to town on Saturdays for business and play. Mom said every Friday night while she lived in Stigler, Oklahoma, her dad took their wagon down to the creek and left it in the water over night to soak the wheels. The wheels were made of wood with a surrounding iron ring. The wood swelled and tightened up enough so the iron rim on the wheel wouldn't fall off the wagon while driving to town on Saturday mornings. Mom said Grandpa took fresh cream they'd separated from the cow's milk each week to town every Saturday morning to sell. Grandpa received about twelve dollars if there was a full can of cream, which was approximately ten gallons. Three dollars was put aside for the up coming week's supply of groceries and another three dollars went towards the mortgage. If enough money was left over, then Mom's brothers Johnny and Jimmy plus Mom and her sister Gurtie, each got a quarter to spend. Mom told us kids how she and her siblings bought four scoops of ice cream each for a nickel, a Royal Crown Cola for a nickel and a half dozen jelly doughnuts, each for a nickel as well. Leaving a dime each, they'd all go to the "Picture Show" and watch the movie that was playing that week. Mom said she'd save the jelly doughnuts to eat while watching the show. She told of "serials," which she also referred to as "cliff hangers." A serial was a half-hour show preceding the movie and was "to be continued" from week to week. This left you "hanging" which made you want to come back and find out what happened next; hence the name "cliff hanger".

After the movie let out, Grandpa returned from whatever business he'd been taking care of and drove everyone home in the wagon to a huge meal that Grandma Jewel had prepared for them while they were gone. Mom said that on Saturdays Grandma cooked up a big ham roast with lots of brown gravy. The gravy was made with the hot ham "drippings" and milk, not with water like we had to fix ours. Grandma boiled corn on the cob and baked two pans of yellow cornbread. Of course there'd be fresh whipped butter and a "batch" of turnip greens. Then Mom told us how she'd take the cornbread and crumble it up to put in her glass of cold milk. I never tired of hearing about the cold fresh milk, and hot yellow cornbread mixed together.

Dad's stories weren't much different than Mom's. Dad's family also sold cream for a living, but in nearby Talihina, which was approximately eighty miles south of Stigler. Dad and Grandpa sometimes spent the day cutting a wagonload of wood to sell in town for a dollar. Eggs collected from Grandma's chickens were not only a source of food for the family, but also brought in some extra spending money. Hogs were raised, butchered, and cured in the smokehouse. Dad said there was no better meat than bacon or ham that came from their smokehouse back home.

When Dad went to town he and his brother Pete rode their horses along with friends from surrounding farms. They also got a quarter to spend every Saturday and they also went to the movies. Dad bought bologna and crackers to take to the movies. He too would buy a

RC Cola, but put a bag of peanuts in before drinking the "pop" as he called the soda.

He told about trying to go to the town dance after the movie, but he was too young to get in. He'd laugh and tell us how he'd let the drunks at the dance ride his horse in trade for shots of whisky. One evening Dad and a friend let one too many drunks ride their horses and they didn't make it home. They stopped along the way and fell asleep on some freshly mowed hay. The two adventurers woke up the next morning with hangovers and frost on their clothes.

~.~.~

I couldn't wait to have a place of our own, so I could ride my horse into town and have fun like Mom and Dad did when they were kids.

I heard these and many other stories at night in the absence of a radio or television. I often fell asleep thinking about being able to have ice cream and jelly doughnuts every Saturday afternoon while at the movies. Naturally, I topped off my fantasy by eating hot smoked ham and crumbled up yellow cornbread in my cold glass of milk for dinner.

~.~.~

I sensed urgency in the voices of my parents and those folks they reminisced with. A short cut back to the bounty of the past was needed, and perhaps the potato fields in Salinas would be a beginning to the road back to paradise.

Even though I hadn't known "the good life" in Oklahoma, the loss of better times my parents suffered sometimes choked me up in a way that almost made me cry. I was only twelve years old and helpless to give them a place to farm. In the back of my mind I thought if I weren't there my parents could more easily regain what they obviously treasured. This made sense to me because there was no more Dust Bowl or Great Depression to blame these hard times on.

~.~.~

After picking cotton all day Saturday, Dad quit his job. We loaded the boat and went to Grandma's for dinner. We visited some and took off for Salinas after Dad had slept for a few hours. It was agreed among the adults that traffic would be lighter driving at night. I thought this different because we usually drove at night, not to keep ourselves cool, but to prevent our old car from overheating due to extra weight from pulling the boat.

Ronnie's sister, Peggy, is sitting in the boat used to haul around their stuff from place to place.

46

5

Valley of Hunger

That Sunday morning our gas gauge read empty as we pulled into a farm labor camp somewhere in the Salinas Valley. It was cold and there was a haunting mist filling the air. My eyes were full of yellow, crusty stuff, and there was no water with which to wash them. I was disoriented having awakened in a strange place, so I asked Dad which way the ocean was and he just pointed. I knew if I faced in the direction of the ocean, north was straight away to my right, and Farmersville was somewhere behind me and perhaps a little south over my left shoulder. We hadn't driven all night, so I knew Farmersville wasn't as far away as Arizona.

I really needed to lie down flat, and to rest free from body parts constantly nudging me. Mom usually kept the baby up in the front seat, which was nice because the rest of us filled the back seat to the point where we overlapped each other. I hurt all over, my skin was dry and itchy, and I'm sure others, had they seen me, would have thought I was having a horribly bad hair day.

Mom was talking with a woman standing in the front of a small white shack with the word "OFFICE" sloppily painted over the front door. She was writing something down on a piece of paper. Then both Mom and the woman walked toward our car. The woman pointed with her cigarette in the direction of where Dad had indicated the ocean was and handed Mom a key. By this time I could see the woman up close through the rear window. She was as tall as my dad, had jet-black hair, and sported a mustache on her upper lip. The smoke from her cigarette faded quickly into the strange mist, which appeared to be hovering only near the ground. She was wearing dark sweat pants, a torn green T-shirt, and pink flip-flops on her feet. The lady too, was having a fairly bad hair day. She seemed nice though, and not at all like she looked.

Mom got back into our car, a pink Rambler Dad bought because the front seats folded back and made out into a bed area. This design was of no help to us kids while driving to a new home.

Mom said, "Drive straight ahead Daddy, to cabin number 44."

I wondered why Mom had said, "cabin" and not house or shack. Could it be there was another, perhaps better part of this camp? By the time I had completed my thought I saw cabin #44. Surely I knew better! It must have been the mist causing me to momentarily lapse into such a fantasyland. Cabin #44 was a shack, which was smaller than most places we'd lived in; it had only one room and it badly needed a whitewashing. Inside there was a bed that smelled of urine, a two-burner electric hot plate, and a sink that had only one faucet.

If we wanted hot water, we had to heat some up on the one burner that worked on the hot plate, and we had to bring water in from outside, because the sink's only faucet didn't work. The faucet leaked though, and there was a large reddish/brown stain in the bottom of the sink. There was no icebox, so we kept perishables in an old number two washtub when we could afford the ice. Not much needed to be refrigerated, with just powdered milk, beans, or perhaps some stale macaroni in the house. If anything needed to be refrigerated, it usually was only one night a week--Saturdays when Dad got paid.

~.~.~

We had an oak icebox with brass handles once, before we moved off and left it somewhere because we had no room to haul it with us. I liked it and thought it was a nice piece of furniture. It made me sad when we had to leave it behind.

~.~.~

We moved in while Dad went to see the crew boss. Moving in was not hard. Mom made the bed after flipping over the mattress in a futile attempt to somehow make it cleaner. I carried in the three or four boxes of free stuff for my sisters to unload. There weren't any drawers or cupboards to unload into, so the boxes were just stacked in a corner.

When Dad returned he told Mom he'd signed us up to work in the potato fields, and we had to be there by 5:30 in the morning. Since the potato field was over twenty miles away, Mom woke me up at 3:30 a.m. and asked if I'd help get the kids ready. She made some Cream of Wheat while I helped dress the smaller children. I put some water on the corner of a towel, held it close to the red-hot coils on the hot plate to warm it a bit, and washed everyone's face.

The Cream of Wheat felt good because it was hot, and this place was colder than most places we had lived in previously. I took hot cups of the white, mushy stuff and gave them to my siblings. Peggy didn't eat any, she just held the cup and warmed her hands. It seemed necessary for me, the eldest, to be the server, because there just wasn't enough room for that many people to move around inside all at once. Everyone needed to stay on his or her own pallet, which was nothing more than a blanket on the floor. I took Steve, who couldn't seem to wake up, to the pee can and sat him down on a pile of clothes before handing him his warm porridge. I sat beside Sandy and held Billie Sue who hadn't yet seen her first birthday. I fed both from the same bowl taking turns spooning in the creamy mush. Dad was outside putting our last gallon of gasoline in the Rambler. I could hear other cars beginning to start up around the camp. I looked outside and saw several headlights shining into the darkness and illuminating the white walls of some of the cabins. Several men were standing around sipping cups of hot coffee with steam rising that reminded me of the time in Springville when Dad had to walk to work.

Irvy said there'd be more good days than bad ones. I thought they were about even to date.

Finally, we were on our way, Mom reading the directions from a piece of torn paper sack, and Dad wiping the dampness off the inside of the windshield with another piece of the same brown bag and finally with the cuff of his shirt. I was comfortable for the first time in a long time. The seat of the Rambler seemed soft, and not at all like the cold, hard floor I'd slept on this same night. The old frayed, checked quilt Mom bought at a second-hand store, where we bought everything, was soft and made us warm, as all five kids were cuddled up underneath it in the backseat. Full of the hot mush and protected from the harsh element outside, I was comfortable in the thought that at least for the next few minutes; no harm would come to me. My eyelids felt heavy and it was hard to keep them open. I covered the side of my face with a corner of the quilt, laid my head against the door and stared out the window at the passing lights.

~.~.~

"Wake up kids, we're here," Mom's voice came from the front seat.

The sight of the potato field was strangely beautiful. Several men wearing overalls, large coats, and straw hats were standing around an old car tire that was on fire near the edge of the roadway. I noticed that nearly everyone was smoking cigarettes and drinking coffee.

As I studied the covey of men, I saw some had their arms crossed with their hands stuck in their armpits. The rest had their arms extended outward away from their bodies, and while exposing the palms of their hands, appeared to be waving to the fire. Many of the men with their arms crossed were shuffling their feet from side to side in the dirt and clicking their heels together in a rhythmic motion. The fellows waving at the fire, all leaning back slightly, were remaining perfectly still except for their hands of course. Everyone had their coat collars turned upward to protect their ears from the frigid outside air.

The fire complemented the red horizon where the sun was just peeking over a hilltop and into the valley. The mist returned and seemed to make things even colder and almost eerie. Dad left the car and disappeared into the gathering of potato pickers. They reminded me of a group of Eskimos all huddled together to keep warm. I saw this once in a National Geographic magazine.

Dad returned with a cup of hot coffee that smelled good enough to eat. He gave anyone a sip that wanted one. Dad told Mom they could start work today, but only got paid for part of this week on Saturday.

Seems that folks worked from Wednesday to Wednesday. Thursday, Friday, Saturday and so on, went on the following weeks check. A bit confusing to me, but Dad seemed to understand, so that made it okay. We had no gas and little food or furniture, so Dad tried, though unsuccessfully, to get a $20.00 cash advance to buy those things we so desperately needed.

Although there wasn't much of a choice, Mom and Dad agreed that since we were already here, we'd stay and give this a try for a couple of weeks. Mom told me to watch the kids, to lock the car doors after they left, and to stay inside until she and Dad returned. Just then I heard a loud noise and saw dark smoke coming out of a rusty pipe sticking out of the top of a big red machine. There were men standing on wooden running boards, one man on each side of the machine, which was being pulled by another man driving a tractor. Mom and Dad fell into cadence behind the flock of pickers and disappeared into the mist.

~.~.~

Several hours later I saw my parents returning to the car. I had already disobeyed Mom twice. I let everyone out of the car to pee at least once each, and I had rolled down the windows, beyond the point that would have stopped an unwanted arm if needed.

"Mom, Dad!" I shouted. "Are we going home now?"

"No, Son," Dad answered. "It's only 11:00 and we can't leave 'till 2:00 o'clock."

I wanted to be good and not cause trouble, but I had spent one too many hours in that car with a bunch of crying, sometimes fighting kids. I was bothered about my retardation; my funny face with awful bucked teeth, being too skinny and wondering if we were going to have enough to eat that day. I worried about having enough sugar water for Billie Sue's bottle, or how we could get more money, or the bully that was for sure going to fight me at my next school, and so on, and on! Dad must have seen the desperation in my face. I truly was at my breaking point.

"Ronnie, take the water bag over to the water truck and fill it with fresh water" Dad said.

Mom said, "David, that water truck is clean acrost the field."

I think Mom must have been worried about so many strangers being around.

Dad didn't answer Mom, he just said without lifting his head, "Go on, Ronnie."

When I returned with the water, I saw that Mom had been crying; seems she did that more and more these days.

The next morning, Dad woke me from where I had slept under whatever table or stick of furniture we had, in this case, an old wooden bench I'd brought in from outside the cabin. I slept under things to prevent from being trampled by a sleepy person trying to find the pee can, or scared "kidlets" trying to get in bed with Mom and Dad because of a bad dream or from being cold.

Dad handed me a biscuit with some apple butter in it. He'd made several for our lunch and said, "Let's go."

He and I left the shack without explanation and got into the back of a pickup with several other men. There were four men in the cab of the truck and I recognized the driver. His name was Buck who was a full-blooded Cherokee Indian. Buck lived near us once in Springville. Buck had several dogs he called "Coon Hounds" and liked to take my dad raccoon hunting at night in the foothills. I liked Buck, and seeing a familiar face made me feel more secure about being in this place.

Photo of Buck and his wife taken in 1961. They are standing at the rear of one of the cabins in the Salinas labor camp.

When we arrived at the potato field, cold wasn't the word to describe how my hands and face felt. My face was hard to the touch, but of course I had no feeling in my fingertips. I remember trying, unsuccessfully, to open and close my hands, and how my fingers hurt when they began to thaw out. Gloves never seemed to be an option, however, I did find a towel and eventually wrapped my hands during the early morning rides.

~.~.~

Dad gave me a leather belt with a thin board attached and connected with two small leather straps. There were two hooks on the bottom of the board hanging in a downward position. Dad told me to strap on the belt, and to let the board hang down in front of me across my legs. Then I was handed a large canvas sack with two brass eyelets at the top edge, which Dad called a potato sack.

I thought potato sacks were made of burlap. We called burlap sacks "toad sacks" or sometimes "gunny sacks." They were "gunny sacks" if we were getting corn at night, and "toad sacks" if we went fishing or "frogging" or catching frogs for their legs. The sacks were called "burlap bags" if we sewed them together to make cotton sacks. Dad took two burlap bags, cut the bottom out of one, and sewed them together forming a tube the length of two or sometimes three sacks. This enabled us kids to fill the lightweight sack with cotton and still be able to drag it along the clod-ridden rows.

Dad told me to take the canvas sack, hang it on the hooks, and let it drag between my legs while I was picking up the potatoes.

Then Dad said, "I'll take two checks and you'll take two checks."

I know I didn't weigh ninety pounds, but I'd never felt bigger than I did at that moment. I was going to be responsible for precisely one half of the family income and I hadn't even reached my teen years yet.

The huge red machine started up. The men along with a few women and young boys like me started to fill in the rows of potatoes about fifty feet apart just so the machine could pass on the left. The sight reminded me of a huge checkerboard with human chess pieces. I thought someone should say, "Ready, set, go!" But no one did.

Just then the tractor pulling the potato-digging machine drove past. The two men on the machine were watching potatoes jump up and down on a wide chain belt, then fall off onto the ground behind the digger. I didn't think those two guys had much to do; besides they laughed too much.

A check was two rows of potatoes about fifty feet long, and after the digger went by, there was a swath of potatoes about six feet wide. The potatoes looked like fish in a stream that had suddenly dried up.

For the next four checks, or two rows of potatoes about 200 feet long, Dad and I had to collect up all the potatoes left behind by the big red machine, and put them into the sacks before the noisy digger came back around again.

"That sack's gonna weigh more than you do, kid," yelled out one of the jokesters from the digger.

I faced in the direction of the jokester and just stared. I didn't understand why a big, burly man was on the machine and not me; it made no sense. I could watch the potatoes jump up and down, and surely the man could pick up potatoes better than I. The man doing nothing was right though; I didn't weigh as much as a full sack of potatoes.

I bent over and continued tossing the potatoes into the sack. Not so bad, I thought. That is until the sack began to fill up, and I started to feel the weight beneath me. I leaned forward hard enough to drag the sack until it was nearly three-quarters full. Then I'd have to stop, prop it up by using one of my hips for leverage, unhook, and run back and forth putting potatoes into the sack until it was full. I filled about three or four sacks per check.

For me, the work was nearly impossible to keep up all day. I had to continue because Mom couldn't for reasons unknown to me, and we needed the money. I couldn't stop because something sad might happen like when those two smelly men took our car away. My body ached at the end of each day, but that was nothing compared to the way I felt when Dad was sad. I saw that Dad was proud of me, and I'd have died before letting him down.

Hard time had befallen my family and me. Desperation was in every breath and survival was paramount. We had few needs other than necessities such as air and water. During lunch break one morning I went to fill our water jar. Dad had taken a quart jar and rapped it with burlap bag fastening it with bailing wire. We'd soak the burlap in water and it seemed to keep the water cooler.

Walking back from the water truck a boy about my age, but bigger approached in an aggressive manner. He was going to take my water away.

"Thank you for getting the water for me. Now let's have it. Hand it over like a good little potato picker," chimed the water bandit.

Air and water were important basic needs to staying alive, something this counter part of mine should have understood. Just as I had felt when the man from the potato picker yelled that the sack was bigger than me, I was surprised at his action and taken off guard unable to reply.

Immediately I was poised to strike and would have defended the jar of water with my life. My body language must have read extreme danger because the thirsty boy threw up both hands.

"Hey man just kidding," he said turning around shaking his head and walking back to his check.

I would have gladly given the boy a drink because we were working too hard for our ages, and I felt a sense of compassion for him. He was new in the potato field and perhaps the pecking order thing was in play here I didn't know. I surprised myself and I think the newcomers as well at my own aggression, ready to do battle to the death over a jug of water.

~.~.~

I learned to beat the cold riding in the back of Buck's truck. I had to, because I never got to ride up front. I remembered how the men crossed their arms to keep warm and how some of them moved and others held still, so I tried some of these techniques. I hunkered down just behind the cab curling up into the baby position, with my forearms tucked between my thighs. I breathed into my cupped hands, which were cradling my face. Later, I also used the towel to turn the harsh cold air away from my face and ears. Then I drifted off into my thoughts.

Sometimes I wondered why Mom quit, but I was afraid to say anything, because I thought it might be a girl thing or something embarrassing like that. Fighting the cold was easier, if I thought about how neat it was going to be when we got our own place.

Dad and I worked together for several weeks that summer, clear past the start of school.

~.~.~

In the evenings, the kids played in the shade of the shack digging in the damp dirt. Chunks of wood became imaginary bulldozers and dump trucks running up and down the play roads in the cool, moist sandy soil.

Saturday afternoons, after everyone had showered, we'd all go grocery shopping and perhaps take a short drive into the countryside.

One bright sunny Sunday morning Mom and Dad loaded us kids up and took us to a nearby second-hand store where we all got new clothes and Mom bought a new washboard. Sandy picked out a frilly thing and a headband of fake roses. That afternoon we put on our new clothes and took a ride in the country. We saw a sign that read, "Petting Zoo--Adults $1.50--Children Under Twelve Free." Well, Mom took us through while Dad rested in the Rambler. He'd parked under a shade tree, rolled down the windows and folded the seats back in order to lie back and catnap. I was glad he could rest, because he worked too hard all the time.

Ronnie holding Billie Sue, then Sandy, Steve and Peggy on the right, posing in front of an animal exhibit at a free petting zoo.

Dad generally took out his guns on the weekends and oiled them up. We had a .410 shotgun, a Marlin .22-caliber rifle, and a Smith and Wesson nine shot .22-caliber pistol with maroon plastic grips. The shotgun belonged to Dad's brother Leonard Jr., or Pete, a nickname given him as a child that stuck. We called him Uncle Pete. He didn't have much use for a shotgun being in the Navy. The rifle had belonged to Dad's younger brother, Ed, before the motor scooter accident in 1959.

Dad was careful not to scratch the guns and kept them wrapped up in old towels and stored under his bed or locked in the trunk of our car if we weren't home. He'd also soap up the tack, or saddles, bridles, or anything made of leather we owned at the time.

Dad cleaned his guns in the house and never outside where they might be seen by other residents of the camps. He did, however, take the tack outside on Sunday afternoons. He'd lay everything out on the hood of our car, straightening each strap of leather flat against the warm metal surface. Dad took an old sock and slipped it over his left hand and dipped the sock into a can of saddle soap, which he kept stored in a small pair of saddlebags. An hour or so later he'd wipe off the excess soap and store the cowboy gear away for another week or so.

Most evenings while the kids played, adults sat around on old fruit boxes drinking sweet tea and talking. Several of the men squatted down on their haunches for hours and smoked hand-rolled cigarettes one after the other. Sometimes after payday some of the men smoked "tailor-mades," or store bought cigarettes.

One evening some folks who had arrived from the grape fields near where my Grandparents lived in the valley, told us about a man there that was trying to help folks like us. I liked anyone who wanted better for me. His name was Cesar Chavez and I wished him well.

Many of the people we met had once owned places back home, some in Oklahoma, some in Arkansas, Texas, New Mexico and so on. The conversation under some sort of shade, most always turned into stories about back home and the places they once loved.

I noticed many of the stories were told multiple times, and were similar in body. Once you were told a "back home" story, it was like gaining acceptance into an exclusive club. Male bonding began with the swapping of stories about their youth in their respective birthplaces.

Most stories spoke of simpler times, times when a penny was worth a penny. A time when all you needed was some tobacco and a horse drawn buckboard wagon to get to town on Saturdays to sell cream or to buy supplies. When a man's word was truly his bond and a time when a handshake sealed most contracts. Many stories included prideful statements such as; "We never took welfare" or "People were always willing to help each other back then." Nearly every story of times "back home" told of a full pantry of preserved or canned foods, which were often referred to as "put up" foods. I remember some of Mom's friends telling me they'd "put up" some peaches, or "put up" some meat in jars to save for "leaner" times.

Very little time was spent talking about how anyone was going to get another "place". I don't recall ever hearing anything negative about when people were living on their places back home in Oklahoma, Texas, or any other state from which folks might have migrated. Everyone we knew had gone from good times in some state to the east, to despair living in tents or their cars in California.

The longer I sat and listened to these stories, the more intent I became on looking ahead into the future. I saw anguish on the faces of the storytellers at the mere mention of what might lie ahead of them in the next year. For the men, it seemed as though living in the past was less hurtful. They enjoyed being with men of similar backgrounds so they could relate to each other more easily. To look past the present was an embarrassment. This meant accepting a hefty dose of reality. To think about having to labor in the fruit or vegetable fields for life, didn't exist for the storytellers if they continued thwarting all thoughts that might lead to the truth. This kind of denial kept them locked solid in the past and was their way of coping with the present.

Women were different though. Overhearing the ladies often brought stories of grandkids attending Sunday dinners at grandmas with their successful mom's and dad's. Their stories, unlike their male partners, were full of hope and futuristic thought.

One dark evening, I was sitting on a log late at night, long past my bedtime, listening to the adults telling stories of their pasts. I fell asleep and dreamed I was in Oklahoma. I needed to go to town to sell my garden produce. I hooked my horse to a dilapidated automobile and steered it while the horse pulled my vehicle loaded down with corn and watermelons to market. When I woke up I was confused. I wasn't able to separate my parent's childhood from mine. I decided right then I was going to take Irvy's advise, listen to everyone, and use only the parts I thought most helpful to me in becoming successful.

Days in the camp eventually seemed to run together. Get up before daylight, eat a biscuit with apple butter and take a freezing ride to the potato fields in the back of Buck's truck. After I thawed out, I wrestled sack after sack of spuds weighing more than me for eight or nine hours, go home, sit in the shade listening to "back home" stories and go to bed hungry.

The only thing different from the day-to-day routine was coming home from working in the fields at noon on Saturdays and not having to get out of bed before sunrise on Sundays. I noted too, other kids my age had gone back to school and the mornings were getting colder.

One very cold Tuesday morning, I woke up because I had to go to the bathroom. As I was trying to locate the pee can, I noticed Dad was gone and it was light outside. Mom was up, humming a country western tune and fixing the last little bit of the oatmeal for our breakfast. She was also patting out some dough. I liked the fried bread she made; we called it "hard tack." It was nothing more than flour and salt mixed with a tad bit of water and pressed out thin like a tortilla. She'd heat the wafer-like spheres in a frying pan until they were hard like crackers. Sugar was sprinkle on top with margarine if we had some. I liked the way our house smelled when Mom made hard tack. Mom seemed to be using up everything we had to eat in the house. I looked at Mom and asked, "Where's Dad?"

"He went to get his check," replied Mom. "We're going to Pop's."

Mom always called Grandma's house "Pop's" or "Len and Nancy's." I heard a car pull up outside and looked out the window. It was Dad. His face was long and he looked very worried. Dad walked into the cabin and over to where Mom was standing in front of the hot plate, where it rested on top of two vegetable crates pushed together with a cloth draped over the top to form a small table.

"Them bastards wouldn't give me my paycheck," growled Dad. "They said to come back Saturday."

I will never forget Mom's disappointment. She quit humming and with the backside of her right hand, pushed her long brown hair to one side and sat down on a wooden fruit box.

"We ain't got no food or money to buy gas with to get to Len and Nancy's," snapped Mom. "What the hell are we supposed to do?" Her voice more matter of fact now.

I was shocked and scared. I'd never heard either of my parents use cuss words. I felt sick inside just like the time when I learned I was going to be starting school the very next day.

"We'll make it, Mother," replied Dad, noting Mom's desperation. "I brought a sack of potatoes with me. We'll eat them and get by." Dad continued, "They're potato-chip potatoes, big and round and they're suppose to taste better than regular ones."

Mom stood up and exploded, "David, what about the baby? We're completely out of powdered milk and we ain't got no sugar for her bottle!" Mom started to cry.

I backed to the opposite side of the bed where Peggy and Steve were already crying because of the loud voices in the room. I picked up Sandy and put her on the bed with the baby. I wanted to cry and probably would have if Dad hadn't been in the room.

"We'll make it, Mother," Dad said. "We've been worse off before. At least we have food." He was trying to be reassuring after Mom's outburst.

"Saturday's pert' near a week away," sobbed Mom. "I don't know David, I just don't know."

Mom left, and I followed her. I wanted to stay with Dad, but by now my stomach was churning inside and I thought being outside might help the sickness go away. I also was scared for my mom. Her father had committed suicide a couple of years earlier. He'd shot himself one evening while sitting in his easy chair at home in Springville.

Once, while holding a kitchen knife, Mom looked at me and said she should just kill herself. I never told Dad and certainly not the little ones. I didn't much believe her, but it worried me from time to time, especially when she got upset.

We never talked about grandpa killing himself, but seeing Mom in this upset state of mind worried me to the point I needed to go with her and leave the little ones with Dad.

Mom went from one cabin to the next, asking for some powdered milk or some sugar. I was in disbelief of Mom's actions. She didn't discuss this with anyone, which wasn't the way she and Dad did things. I felt horrible and an attack of diarrhea was coming on.

No one could help, weren't willing to share, or just plain didn't have anything to share. I hated to see Mom beg for food, which added to my despair, but I supposed I'd have done the same thing had I been in her shoes.

After knocking at a front door, the lady of the house surrounded by curious dirty faced children answered and looked at Mom. I had learned to read peoples eyes and could see the women understood what Mom was going to say before she said it. Asking for food wasn't that uncommon, it was just new to us. One lady didn't even wait for Mom to ask, she said, "Oh sweetie, I don't have anything left over, I'm so sorry." She closed the door in front of us, leaving Mom without ever having said a word.

Most everyone offered to give us potatoes, but we already had a supply for the week. I wanted to tell everyone they were potato chip potatoes, the big round good kind, but I didn't. None of the families we visited had any sugar or powered milk to offer.

When Mom and I returned to our cabin, I noticed Mom and Dad didn't say anything to each other. The little ones were playing as if nothing had happened. Billie Sue seemed unhappy though. Perhaps the routine of drinking sugar water demanded a refill, and not having any made her cranky.

That night, a black woman brought over two cans of condensed milk with a small sack of sugar and gave them to Mom.

"Here honey, I know the pain of putting a baby to bed without its bottle," she whispered. Her eyes were warm and reassuring.

Mom stared for a moment, and said, "Thank you."

"God bless you and good luck," the women said before she turned in the direction of the office and walked away into the darkness.

The life giving items were in a grocery bag as if she'd just brought them straight from the store.

My stare had been frozen to the woman's face. Her smile was soft and friendly. Her skin glistened in the light streaming out from the kitchen. She wore a dark blue dress with white polka dots and carried a shinny black purse on her left forearm. She was wearing a string of white pearls around her neck. That alone told me she wasn't a resident of our camp. I was surprised to see her because Mom and I had not spoken to any black folks; as a matter of fact, we'd never spoken to a black person.

Billie Sue had been cranky and refused to nurse her bottle with only water in it. As soon as Mom added a little of the canned milk to the bottle, Billie's eyes almost immediately drooped and looked heavy; she soon fell fast asleep.

Dad spent several hours that night sitting on the front step smoking and staring at the other side of the camp. This reminded me of an old photograph we kept of my great grandparents. The photo showed my dad's grandparents sitting out front of their cabin in Pixley, after arriving from Oklahoma. The elderly babysat the young, while all able-bodied folks worked in the fields. Furniture had been moved outside where the men slept to give the women and children more room inside at night.

Sometime later Dad's parents settled in Farmersville after Grandpa got a job as grounds keeper with the Exeter Cemetery District, which included an older Deep Creek Cemetery near Farmersville. It didn't seem that life had changed too much for Dad, and remembering the old photograph made me wonder what was going through his mind.

Photo of my great grandmother "Ronie." She was Cherokee Indian. Great Grandpa Anderson is sitting in the background wearing his hat. They're visiting with a neighbor that's leaning on the old truck.

That week we ate potatoes fried, mashed, hashed, boiled, baked, peeled, not peeled, and stripped, which was what we called French fries if we were eating them at home.

~.~.~

Receiving commodities or welfare was never an option for us except on one occasion. Dad had an ulcer rupture and was off work for several weeks. When I was nine we lived in a small community called Alta Vista just outside Porterville, California, where I attended the third grade for a while. My grandmother came to our house one day and took me with her to pick up commodities. We drove to Visalia about thirty minutes northwest and stood in line at an old train station across the street from the jail; I was so embarrassed I stared at the ground and refused to look up. Commodities were flour, sugar, powdered milk, canned meat and beans. Not too much different from what we bought when we had money and went to the grocery story, except commodities were free. At first I was happy about the canned meat because I liked Spam so much. I was soon to realize that all canned meat wasn't alike. The meat was like eating wet cardboard that had been retrieved from a mud hole. The really raunchy stuff was the brown gelatin like substance that swirled throughout the layers of the pinkish brown chunks of meat.

My father strongly believed in families taking care of their own. He was very sick recovering from surgery, and I don't think he ever knew about the charity we'd accepted. Other than that day no one ever spoke of the free food again.

Shortly after my father recovered from what turned out to be two surgeries and yet another move, two men wearing suits and ties visited our house. We learned our family had been selected to receive food and presents during the upcoming Christmas Holidays. The two gentlemen were representatives of the Three Rivers Lions Club. I liked living in Three Rivers because it was in the mountains, plus I was doing well in the fourth grade.

A couple of days before Christmas several cars showed up with stuff that was supposed to cheer us up, which included a Christmas tree. My father wasn't at home and I ran and hid until the good Samaritans were gone. The attitude around the house was subdued when Dad got home from his part-time job. He drove away for a few hours and again no one spoke of the free food as we gobbled it up. One of my Christmas gifts contained a pair of briefs. They were the first I'd owned, and I remember it took some time getting accustomed to wearing them.

I was so embarrassed when I returned to my school, thinking that everyone was talking about our Christmas welfare package. In fact, I really didn't know if anyone knew about it at all.

That was the Christmas when I saw Mom and Dad pouring over a medical bill at the kitchen table. Dad told Mom he couldn't pay back the total of the money owed with a lifetime of paychecks and that bankruptcy was their only option.

~.~.~

That week in the camp, having no food in the house and five kids to feed, must have been unbelievably torturous for Mom and Dad. One afternoon Mom set the table and called us kids to eat. We sat down expecting potatoes, but all we got was a glass of water each, and then she shooed us away. Mom washed and dried the dishes and put everything away. I never asked why she did that, but I figured not being able to feed starving children might cause you to do your part, and hope somehow others would do theirs. I believed Mom's actions to be a desperate act of someone in a desperate situation.

I knew I had to somehow do more about our present situation. Seemed to me lives depended on getting more food. We couldn't ask for welfare, and certainly we couldn't rob other folks of their stuff. Perhaps I could find a dump. We use to go to the county dump and rummage through old davenports and easy chairs to locate change. There were no dumps I knew of within walking distance of the camp, so I couldn't do that. I was glad because I never liked rummaging through trash where the rats lived. All I had to do was find enough money to buy a loaf of bread and a half-pound of bologna to get by until payday rolled around.

I felt desperation inside watching Dad sit and stare off into space and Mom pretending to feed us kids while having no food to fix. I knew I had to do something soon to get more food.

~.~.~

Other families in the camp were much worse off than we were. One Hispanic family of ten lived near us. Their cabin was bigger than ours, having twice the space. They had nothing but beds and suitcases in two tiny rooms, and to say they were crowded was an understatement.

To compound matters, a second family of eight from New Mexico moved in. The women and young children stayed in the cabin at night while the older boys and men slept outside in cars and under cardboard boxes. Some slept in our boat and eventually bought it to use as a trailer to haul their stuff around.

It was expected, that the older teenage boys and girls, rotate between staying home and going to school. The boys took turns going to the fields, while the girls took turns babysitting, doing the laundry or tending to other family needs.

I remember one teenage girl, who was maybe two years older than me, had to get up at 3:30 every morning and cook. She and her mother made two hundred fifty tacos over an open fire outside on a disc blade before school. She'd put eggs in some for breakfast and beans in others for lunch. Most of the time this frail little Mexican girl stayed home from school and took care of her baby brothers and sisters who didn't yet attend school. She also babysat for other families whose mothers worked in the fields.

Life in the farm labor camps was difficult, even when everyone did more than their fair share.

I'd decided my brother and sisters needed more to eat, so I came up with a plan.

There was a chocolate factory near the labor camp, and I guess the smell of sweet chocolate drifting in through an open window at night helped in my decision-making.

The idea hit me like a bolt of lightening! I remembered seeing a soda bottle near the railroad tracks once coming back from a nearby grocery store with Mom. I picked up the bottle and sold it for three cents the next time I went to the store.

~.~.~

I'd pretend to be going to the shower house, and to use the toilet, which was clearly a block away from our cabin, and began my plan to feed the little ones. I ran everywhere I went, so I really had to hurry in order to pull this off.

I ran past the shower house, and another couple of blocks over to the train yards, where amazingly enough, I found pop bottles. Maybe the old adage "One man's trash is another man's treasure" has merit.

I had only enough time to find two or three bottles, run to the nearby corner store, cash them in, and get back before being missed. I sold the pop bottles for three cents each and bought two-for-a-penny candy with the money. Of course, I'd have to stick my head under a faucet, to make it look like I'd showered in order to complete the ruse.

When I got back to the cabin, I rounded up the kids and hid between two of the shacks and away from Mom's gaze. My siblings never said a word looking completely astonished at what I'd brought them. Dirty, speechless, disheveled and wide-eyed, they waited for me to give them their share of the goodies.

I bought things like Abba Zabba, licorice, or anything else chewy to make it last. I bought a Big Hunk if it was cold outside. I'd pound the candy against a cold rock and it would shatter into several pieces and could be distributed fairly and evenly to my starving brother and sisters. Warm Big Hunks were really chewy, but hard to tear apart and not easily shared.

Tootsie Rolls were the best. The big ones cost a nickel, but well worth every penny. They already had marked sections, which made it easy to be fair while sharing and they really did last a "long, long, time."

~.~.~

The week passed without having taken a shower, and that was okay with me. Not because I enjoyed the grit around my collar, or because the toilets were communal and grotesque, but because there was an old man that was always following me to the shower house.

The man was tall, much taller than Dad, who always told me he was five feet eleven and three quarter inches tall. He always wore the same clothes, a dirty brown long sleeved shirt and dark blue pants with food stains all over the front. His pants, held up by red suspenders, showed black greasy areas where he placed his hands on them.

His hair was oily and slicked down. It was gray with streaks of yellow. Combed straight back his hair laid close to his head until coming to the nape of his neck, where thick curly hairs stood out beyond his shirt collar. His half inch white whiskers were thin and sparse on a face that looked leathery and weather worn. Deep crevasses sliced through each cheek like washed out ruts in a dirt road. He was exceedingly thin, which accentuated the length of his skinny fingers right down to the tips of his long, filthy and nicotine stained fingernails.

I was frightened of him and I wished he'd leave me alone.

The old man was forever following me, telling me I had no butt. The old guy never touched me, but liked to watch me take showers, and that made me a bit nervous. I never saw him in the potato fields and I was glad about that.

On what turned out to be our last day in the camp, I went to take a shower. I didn't want Dad to know about the old man because I knew that Dad would hit him and probably get into trouble.

When I got to the shower house, there he was standing just outside the entrance and smoking a hand rolled cigarette. I went in, took off my clothes and stepped into one of the gray and dismal showers. There were no curtains to provide privacy and no doors on the toilet stalls directly across from them.

I felt the man's stares when he came into the cold, damp cement room. He strolled sideways over to a toilet, never taking his eyes off me. He pulled down his pants exposing his excitement. He put his hand on himself, sat down and looked up at me with black beady eyes. I looked around the empty room and slowly looked back at the pervert. When our eyes met I started screaming as if the Boston Strangler himself had sat on that grungy toilet. My screams were blood curdling, and every bit as shrill as my sisters were, as I had not yet reached puberty.

The man's cigarette dropped from his mouth and his feet came off the floor as he jumped up struggling to pull up his pants. I saw that his cigarette wasn't the only thing that had dropped. He was still pulling at his suspenders as he ran from the bathhouse.

A minute or so later, two men and a teenage boy rushed through the door.

One of the men questioned, "Are you all right? We heard screaming."

"Yes sir, I saw a rat, but he ran away" I said.

"Okay son, be careful, those damn rats can be pretty mean at times," said the same man as he followed the other would-be rescuers outside.

"Thank you sir, I think I've learned how to handle rats", I replied as I turned off the shower and grabbed my towel.

I felt really good about scarring the old peeper and smiled to myself while walking back to cabin #44.

~.~.~

I made twenty-seven cents, not counting the five-cent Party-Pack bottle I'd found on Thursday. I enjoyed my bottle runs, and remembered the satisfaction it gave me to watch my brother and sisters get their candy.

~.~.~

We had no gas, and no money to buy any. I suggested we go find pop bottles to sell or trade in for gas. My parents thought this was a good idea, and that's exactly what we did. This enabled my dad to drive and get his paycheck, instead of catching a ride with Buck in the morning and hitchhiking back as he'd planned.

The next morning was Saturday, so Dad left early to go get his check. He took a kitchen knife with him and told Mom not to worry. She could rest assured he'd come back with his money one way or another.

This week had been unlike any other in my life. Mom and Dad had sworn in front of us kids and now my father was taking a knife with him to get his paycheck. Times were hard, but we did have potatoes to eat and we weren't sleeping outside in cardboard boxes like the Mexicans next door.

When Dad returned, he had his paycheck and exciting news of a new job. He'd gone to the unemployment office on his way home. Apparently he'd met a rancher there, and had gotten a job on a ranch in Panoche Valley in the foothills east of Hollister.

We packed the Rambler and headed for the nearest grocery store to buy "fixins" for bologna sandwiches. The plan was to eat bologna sandwiches in the car on the way to our new home.

Before Dad went into the store, he asked us kids what we wanted to eat and took our orders. I ordered a cherry pie, a Zero candy bar, and a 10-2 & 4 to drink.

Dad left, went into the store, and a short time later came out carrying two brown grocery bags. He leaned inside the car pushing the bags across the front seat to Mom and said, "Here, Mother, pass this out while I put a couple of bucks in the tank." Mom gave me two cherry pies, two Zero candy bars, and two Dr. Pepper's to drink. Dad had doubled every order.

We headed out for Panoche and a new beginning. Mom made bologna sandwiches in the front seat, and I made sure all the little ones had their food and opened everyone's drink. While ripping the paper off the top of my cherry pie, I leaned back against a potato that had been left behind there in the back seat. I grabbed up the spud and held it out the window to toss it, but couldn't let go. I stared at the round tan*ish* colored tuber momentarily, and retrieved it, placing it gently on the floor next to my feet.

I put the exposed icing covered pastry in my mouth and closed my eyes. Every single solitary bite was totally, beyond the shadow of a doubt and to a moral certainty, glorious!

~.~.~

Panoche Valley was nestled in the Diablo Mountains a few miles west of what I'd always known as my security blanket, the San Joaquin Valley, and about thirty miles east of Hollister. The ranch was over 15,000 acres big and pushed up into the southeast corner of the valley. It was known as the "Old Curtner Ranch."

All but about two hundred acres were leased out as grazing land to the White Cattle Company. Dad was to farm alfalfa and to grow a new crop being introduced to the area known as safflower, a white grain encapsulated in a thistle head used in making cooking oil. There was a older rundown house and a barn near a creek, room for a cow, a horse, and some chickens. There was space for a garden to grow things for Mom to "put up" in jars. There was a creek, but it only ran water during the winter. No fish, but very nearly the perfect place.

I stood out by the barn and looked at the picturesque surroundings. I realized that there was going to be wild game, like rabbits, deer, and pheasants. The best thing about all of this, was that they were all edible.

Yes, this might just be "the place".

6

The Corral Fence

As I stood out by the barn leaning on a corral board, I was overcome with emotion. I had endured much without realizing it. I simply thought that life was a bitch and then you died; that there were only two classes of people, the "haves" and those like us, the "have nots." There was no middle ground for me at this point in my life. I was having trouble believing something good was happening to my family and me. I stayed in denial for weeks, not believing or trusting such a place existed, and I was actually living there.

I was especially happy for my brother and sisters, because I didn't have to worry about them so much. For the first time in our lives, we could go out and play without the fear of running into some dirty, beady eyed, old man giving us weird stares, sitting on the pot for all the camp to see, or keeping an eye out for the neighborhood bully.

My sister Peggy read in the pleasant surroundings of a backyard shade tree, with only the nearby sounds of feeding sparrows. Steve sewed contently on 4-H projects now. With this much space available, Sandy, my middle sister, rode horses and could shoot guns with the boys. Billie Sue was still a toddler, but played on a clean floor free of hazardous splintery holes or sharp cement corners. Her bottle was full of real milk most of the time and she seemed to cry less.

This was a happier place for Mom as well and I was glad about that. Dad was truly in his element, and worked with a straightforward focus, an almost vengeful drive to succeed. He was enjoying life here and even walked more upright.

~.~.~

The setting in Panoche was one of enormous space. I could shoot a .22 rifle in almost any direction and not worry about hitting anyone, because there were so few people in the area. The mid-sized hills surrounding the ranch afforded terrific hunting.

There were two large hay fields and equipment with which to farm them. The house was small, but it had an indoor toilet! It wasn't our first indoor toilet, but it was the best, having hot and cold running water and a huge white bathtub that stood on eagles' feet.

~.~.~

The first porcelain toilet we had was inside a rustic rundown wooden outhouse we used when I was about seven years old. I remember wanting to have friends sleep over, so I could show them our new flush toilet. It was so wonderful, not to have to go to the outhouse and see a black widow spider scurrying out of sight, just six inches beneath the hole where you were about to sit.

Resting inside a dilapidated outhouse, the white porcelain toilet stood as a testament to a better life for us. It signified a step up to a higher rung on the ladder of life my family had been slowly climbing for many years. Each rung was a struggle, some breaking, some not, but each step up gave us hope to move on toward the "good life" that we sought out with such drive and sacrifice.

"I wanted to have my friends sleep over and show them our new porcelain flush toilet."

The house in Panoche hadn't been lived in for years and was incredibly dirty. Mom and Dad boiled water and threw it on the walls to clean them.

Cockroaches were abundant! Dad sprayed the house one day with an old Black Flag pump sprayer to kill the roaches. The next morning I opened the sink cupboard doors and found over two solid inches of dead cockroaches.

I spent a lot of time leaning and sitting on the corral fence by the barn that was shaded by a huge cottonwood tree. The view overlooked the tree-lined riverbed cutting its way through the valley.

Rows of cottonwood trees had been planted years earlier as windbreaks, and they framed the foothills in the background. The green hay fields across the creek sat on the alluvial fan that poured out toward the riverbank at the base of the now green hills, which paralleled the blue-sky horizon.

While at the corrals, I remembered things happening in my life that seemed strangely distant. Five years earlier, my second grade teacher told Mom I was retarded. I'd stayed quiet and stopped eating to the point where I almost died. A couple of years of not eating enough and not having enough to eat left me weak and lifeless.

The corral fence became my refuge. A spot where I slowed down, and took the time to find rationalization of events past and present.

Sometimes I'd do nothing more than fantasize about having a place like the one back home, and how neat it'd be to have a swimming hole with snakes in it. Or, perhaps having a creek that ran into a pond full of fish. If I got hungry, all I'd have to do was to catch a fish and have Mom cook it up. Thoughts of "simpler times" like these made me happy, and I wondered why attaining such a place had to be so difficult.

I also thought about a girl at my new school. I'd thought about girls before, but never with such persistence.

Her name was Jeannette. She was an only child and lived with her parents on a ranch about three miles west of our house. She was in the sixth grade, one grade behind me. Of course she never noticed me, but I couldn't help noticing her. She had the most beautiful jet-black hair I'd ever seen and always wore the prettiest dresses. As wonderful as I thought she was, I couldn't come up with enough "gumption" to talk to her.

When I was around Jeannette I became keenly aware of my bucked teeth. The older I got the more my teeth protruded from my face. I'd taken a lot of ribbing in my earlier years, but now they were becoming an embarrassment and caused me more pain than the ribbing. Because of my shyness, I had to admire Jeannette from afar.

I often thought of Jeannette before going to sleep at night. I thought about how wonderful it might be to share a lunch with her, or perhaps to study our spelling words together. In either fantasy I'd get to sit close to her and to be near her was what I really wanted.

~.~.~

Mainly, I remembered how much the hunger hurt. It wasn't just the physical pain, but the emotional pain as well. The pain I got in my sides when I was hungry, wasn't anything compared to the sadness I felt when I saw my father's face when we had no food, or the puzzled looked in my sisters' eyes when they needed to eat and nothing was available to them. These kinds of thoughts raced through my head there at the isolated corral, and I realized they were permanently burned into my memory.

Hunger has no boundaries, cultural or otherwise. I had gotten to know the pangs of hunger on a first-name basis. Some of the names that came to mind were malicious, torturous, relentless and agony--to name a few. I remembered the mental and physical pain that suffering from hunger causes, and I vowed to never, ever forget.

7

Tobacco Juice

I spent a lot of time around the barn. I built a chicken coop for the six White Leghorn hens and a Rhode Island Red rooster we bought one Sunday morning at a flea market in Hollister. I kept the chickens in a wire, wood framed rabbit pen for two days while I built the coop. I put on a partial roof and some roosts underneath for the chickens to get in out of the weather and up off the ground at night. I built a row of wooden boxes on the outside of the coop with a hinged top, so I could collect eggs without having to walk inside the coop. I so enjoyed doing the stuff Dad did as a child.

Sandy with her bike, standing in front of the chicken coop that Ronnie build next to the barn in Panoche Valley.

I took a shovel and spaded up a large garden spot behind the small tool shed, located a short distance north of the barn. Several tall shade trees surrounded the shed, which made a pleasant place to make repairs on our farming equipment.

In early spring, I planted corn, tomatoes, okra, carrots, beets, onions, and squash. I didn't plant a single potato because I was sick of them. By this time, I was gathering a couple of eggs a day.

Dad bought a red pig, which we named Libby. Dad said the pig was a Duroc sow, and if she had babies there'd probably be a large litter because she was a Duroc. Libby was a good find because she was pregnant and we'd soon have little piglets to raise for more meat.

Summer was just around the corner when Libby gave birth to only three piglets.

Ronnie posing for a photograph with his Duroc Sow "Libby."

School was about to let out for the next three months. I liked my school in Panoche, because it was small and quaint. It was a one-room schoolhouse. Inside there was a stage on one side of the room, and a large six-brick heater near the teacher's desk on the other. I'd been told about a very large black potbellied stove that used to heat the school. I often thought it'd be great to have a wood-burning stove to heat us like in the olden days.

Panoche School as it looked in 1960. Photo provided by Margaret Strohn.

There was one teacher at the school. His name was Mr. Light. Mr. Light was short and stocky, and his hair was thinning dramatically. Less than twenty children populated the whole school and four of them were Hughart kids. The offspring of a half dozen families made up the student body both years I attended Panoche School.

There was a smaller school a few miles to the west called Emmet School. There often were only one or two families in attendance each year. When we went on field trips the student or students from Emmet would go with us.

Panoche and Emmet Schools--Classes of 1964 on a field trip to San Juan Batista Mission. Left to right:

Top row--Paige Fancher-Emmet School, Johnny Light peeking around his Dad's head, Mr. Light looking as if his chin is in Jeannette's hair, Katie Fancher-Emmet School- she's wearing the dark glasses, Larry Vanderford, Ronnie and Millard Strohn.

Middle row--Pattie Magorian, Michael Rey, Jeannette Velasquez, My sister-Peggy Hughart with her new glasses, Duane Magorian, Mark Fancher-Emmet School, and Dudley Stewart nearly being cut out of the photo.

Front row--Donald "Corkie" Magorian, My brother,-Steve Hughart looking smug, Leslie Fancher Emmet School and in the white sweater is Nedra Light.

Not shown: Georgia and Peter Strohn, Melanie and Janelle Light and my sister Sandy. Photo provided by Jeannette Velasquez.

Mr. Light taught several grade levels, kindergarten through the eighth grade. He was a teacher, 4-H leader, coach, woodshop instructor, and a person everyone in the community turned to for advice and friendship. He was always willing to give his all.

On the weekends Mr. Light sometimes came to our house, where he'd pick me up to go chucker hunting. He'd bring a shotgun he kept in a brown cloth case and I'd take Dad's .410 gauge. We'd drive to the foothills located at the back of the ranch and walk through the canyons and gullies watching for chucker, a type of grouse. I liked hunting with Mr. Light because he praised me when I shot one of the pheasant-like birds on the fly.

I was thirteen and a half now and looking forward to summer break in this peaceful place.

Mr. Light, Ronnie's eight-grade teacher, is sitting at his desk near the six brick heater in the one room schoolhouse in 1963.

That summer between my seventh and eighth grade years, I got a job building fence in the melon fields near Firebaugh. Jim, a cowboy who lived nearby and worked on the ranch, hired me for the summer. Jim was in his forties, almost as wide as he was tall, and as strong as a bull. I was told that Jim had "rodeoed" in his younger years and was quite good at it. He later taught me how to bulldog a steer.

Jim drove us to the melon fields where we met a young man in his twenties. We built fences using iron pickets and barbed wire to surround melon fields. Cows were brought in to feed on the over ripened melons left behind by the pickers. When the melons were all gone, we three fence builders had already enclosed another field. The cows were moved to the new field and we'd tear down the old fence. So went the rest of the summer.

Once in a while, a new roll of barbed wire had to be rolled out. It was not unusual to fence a melon field that was a mile square, so it was not at all unusual to use four miles of wire to enclose one field. Jim took a crowbar, slipped it through the new roll of wire and connected the bar to the back of his pickup bed.

One day I was riding in the back of Jim's truck watching the wire roll out as Jim drove slowly forward. The wire hung up and I instinctively grabbed at it. That was a serious mistake, because when the wire let go, it took my gloved hand with it. I screamed, and yelled for Jim to stop! Before he could step on the brakes, the wire had dug large holes into the flesh of my left arm. Jim stopped and came to my aide. He always chewed tobacco and told me to hold out my arm. Before I realized what was happening, Jim had spit my wounds full of tobacco juice. Wiping the brown residue from his chin, Jim told me his father had taught him the tobacco juice remedy for healing wounds. Sure enough, my arm never even got sore, and it healed well.

~.~.~

As summer's curtain closed and fall fell into position, I entered the eighth grade. I had also worked with Dad in the hay fields that summer. I often baled hay at night before going to build fence with Jim during the day.

On one occasion while helping my father in the hay fields, I came close to losing my life... too close. There had been several dry nights in a row and if the morning dew failed to come in, we weren't able to bale the hay. Early morning dew dampened the alfalfa and prevented the leaves from falling off their stems, which was imperative when baling hay. Dad rigged up a small watering tank with an attached piece of pipe drilled full of holes. The perforated pipe was sticking out from the tank about four feet, and the whole thing rested on a harrow bed just behind the driver.

A harrow bed is a machine that is used in picking up and stacking bales of hay. The driver sits out beyond the front tires about six to eight feet. This was a homemade harrow bed and the driver sat at least eight feet forward of the front axle.

I was to take the harrow bed, open the rigged faucet releasing the flow of water from the pipe that jutted out over the windrows or rolled up rows of hay, and drive slowly along to wet the alfalfa. This moistened the hay just enough, so it could be baled up without losing too many of its leaves. I had helped like this in the hay fields for several nights in a row and I was very, very, tired.

The creek was lined with vertical dirt banks. Over the years the river cut into the valley floor about thirty feet or so. As I was driving along about three o'clock in the morning down one of the windrows of hay, and heading in the direction of the creek, my head fell forward. I opened my eyes into total darkness! I slammed on the brakes and looked into nothingness! The void seemingly had no top or bottom as I struggled to focus my eyes.

The ground that should have been under the machine simply wasn't there. My headlights showed nothing at all in front of me, and I knew I was in really big trouble. Although disorientated, I saw the lights of the bailer coming into view a few yards behind me and decided to back up. While backing, I saw the edge of the creek bank come into view in my headlights. My front tire marks were explicit evidence to my near tragedy and had actually rounded off the top edge of the dirt bank.

I'd been suspended some seven and a half feet out over the vertical cliff. Six inches further, a couple tons of steel would have dropped right on top of me. I continued to wet the hay until morning, then I went to build fence with Jim for the last time that summer. I never told my parents of the riverbank incident. I didn't tell because I liked driving the farm equipment. If I told

Mom and Dad they might be scared to the point they wouldn't let me drive anymore.

Ronnie driving the homemade harrow bed out to the alfalfa field to load bales of hay.

There was one other close call while living in Panoche. My brother Steve and I had joined the 4-H Club and I was fixing up the front yard as a project. I built a fence around a new lawn and a couple of cherry trees I'd planted. Jim's wife, Dolly, gave me a couple of rose bushes to help add some color and I'd built a rock wall to stair step where the hill fell sharply into the yard.

Working in the cool of the evening was best and that's usually when I was out in the front. It was after dinner about dusk while piling river rock on top of each other when the close call happened.

First, I heard what sounded like a bee off in the distance. Before I could look up I thought a firecracker had gone off in my right ear. Then the bee sound came again, only this time the sound was rapidly fading away in the opposite direction.

I went inside the house and told Mom what had happened and that my ear was ringing. She looked and told me the hair above my right ear was burned and refused to let me go back outside. Apparently a bullet had come close enough to my head to singe my hair.

My father went down to the creek to see if possibly hunters were poaching rabbits, but couldn't find anything.

I was a bit uncomfortable the next few times I worked out front, but soon got over the scare and wrote the incident off as a fluke.

Ronnie is working on his 4-H project in the front yard of the old house in Panoche. He is standing in the exact spot where a bullet singed his hair a few days earlier.

8

Cricket

There were four eighth-grade boys in my school that year. Dwayne the quiet one, Larry the daredevil, Peter the redhead, and me. If all of us graduated, it would beat the record number of students graduating from the eighth grade in a single year, in all of the ninety-one-year history of Panoche School. If I got to stay at this school all year, it would be the longest stay in a single school for me. I liked it here and hoped we didn't have to move.

Soon after the start of school, I arrived home to find a very skinny dark brown mare tied up to one of the cottonwood trees near the ranch's tack room. The small horse had long shaggy brown hair and overgrown hooves that desperately needed trimming. Dad walked by and said, "Bought her for your summer's work." I knew he meant the mare was my paycheck for the summer.

Starved and confused, the little mare came to Panoche Valley in much the same condition as I did some ten months earlier. It was love at first sight. This was too perfect. We had a house and a barn near a creek, chickens to tend, a garden full of stuff for Mom to "put up" and now a horse to ride. There were cows on the ranch, so we now had everything but fish in the creek and snakes to swim with.

Dad's horse back home had been named Cricket, so of course, the only name for my new little mare was Cricket. I was excited at the thought of training her.

First, I put her on a lunge-line, which was a length of rope about twenty feet long attached to her halter. I made her trot in circles around me to the right and then to the left. After a day or so of this I did the same thing, except I put a saddle on her before trotting her around in the corral. At the end of each session on the lunge-line, I snubbed her, or tied her to a post and let her "soak", or stand with the saddle on for a couple of hours. This helped her get use to the feel and sounds of the saddle.

Even though I really never saw Dad watching, I knew he was monitoring my progress. There was no need to watch me; after all I was going to turn fourteen on the 22nd of this month. The only thing Dad said to me was to take the mare out to the plowed field and get on her before she got all her strength back. Shortly after Dad gave me his advice, I took Cricket across the creek to the plowed field.

While still at the tack room I took off her halter and strapped it around her neck, so if she pulled away I could grab the lead rope, which was attached to her halter, and stop her. Then I put the bridle on Cricket's head and she took the bit in her mouth without much trouble. I grabbed up a saddle blanket and placed it gently on her shoulder, then rubbed it slowly onto her back. I had done this a couple of times before and Cricket seemed to be okay with it. Lastly, I picked up the saddle and folded the right stirrup back over the seat, so I could place it gently on top of Cricket's back. I'd not saddled Cricket out in the open outside the corral. So far, so good!

Ronnie's horse Cricket saddled for the first time outside the corral.

I cinched the saddle and took off the halter from Cricket's neck. I walked my pony around in a circle for a minute or two and re-cinched the saddle because she had bloated up. Not really taking in air, swelling her belly, or bloating up as we called it, but tensing up to the point that when she relaxed, the saddle loosened, so it was always a good idea to cinch up a second time before getting on your horse.

I put split reins on the bridle so I could hold each rein out to one side and "plow-rein" or pull hard on either the right or left side to turn her more easily if needed.

I wondered how all this was going to turn out as I lead Cricket in one last circle. I must admit I was just a little nervous and wondered if I was brave enough to get on. I lead Cricket the half mile to the plowed field thinking the walk would help her get used to the saddle before I got on.

The moment of truth at last! I pulled Cricket's head toward me with the left rein. Keeping the rein short I grabbed the saddle horn with two hands as I placed my left foot into the left stirrup. I murmured, "I hope to see fourteen." I pulled up and centered my weight over my horse's withers, swung my right leg across the saddle and sat down. I clenched my knees hard against the swell of the old Jumbo saddle and nothing happened. Cricket was not moving! My mind was racing. What had I done wrong? Was I up to this challenge? I made myself think through this situation and decided to make the first move, be it right or wrong. There was no turning back at this point for me. I was now willing to risk life and limb to ride this animal. I knew my father wouldn't say anything, but this was the one thing he'd be most proud of me for doing.

I began to plow rein Cricket to the left and kicked her ever so slightly. Cricket lunged straight forward. I pulled harder to the left and she circled taking huge jumps sidewise across the plowed surface. Three circles and I plowed her to the right. A few circles later I tried to stop my steed. She would not stop! Each time I tried to stop, she bucked with me. I circled to the left again and then to the right for what seemed like a half-hour. I tried stopping several times to no avail. Finally, it was like Cricket suddenly got it, she lowered her head, snorted the dirt beneath her and stopped. I tugged on the reins lifting her head and rode Cricket down the middle, well, sort of down the middle of the road all the way home. Mom and Dad saw me ride Cricket into the barnyard and I felt very proud.

Cricket improved half again as well each day after that, and in a week, was considered to be in cowboy language, a "broke" horse.

About a week later, late one afternoon I decided I was going to ride Cricket down in the dry creek bed. At first she walked through the trees quite well and trotted the same. A gallop was next and then Cricket decided running would also be fun. I thought, why not. I gave her head and dropped the reins to see how fast she could run. This turned out to be a wrong decision. Cricket took the bit clinching it in her teeth, put her head down, and ran away with me hanging on the best I could. I tried to turn her but too late, a limb came out of nowhere just like Mr. Hot Shit, a new name I'd given the eighth grade King of the Hill, who came out of nowhere with his goons back in the fifth grade. The limb caught the saddle horn slamming me into the vertical dirt wall just to my left. I got up and stumbled after my horse. A short piece down the trail I found my mount with the saddle still attached but hanging beneath her belly.

Dad had always told me when a young man got his first new car, he'd have to see what it would do, meaning how fast it'd go. Dad also pointed out this was the time a young man was most probably going to get into trouble or worse.

That night at dinner, I looked at my father and said, "Dad, you were right about not speeding." I knew he had seen the damage done to my saddle horn made by the tree limb. Dad just smiled and nodded.

Our mailbox was two miles east at the "Y" in the road with about a half dozen other mailboxes. If you turned to the right, you'd be going in the direction of the school. Turn left and Jeannette's house was about a quarter mile down and on the left-hand side.

Our mail arrived three days a week; on Mondays, Wednesdays and Fridays. It came from the Paicines General Store, which doubled as a post office twenty-five miles away to the east. We ordered supplies on Monday and if we wanted, could have them delivered with the mail on following Wednesday or Friday.

After the last episode with Cricket, I decided to take it easy and do more things like riding her safely to the "Y" to get the mail. Dad made a set of saddlebags so I could more easily carry the letters and groceries back to the house.

Many times I wanted to ride on and visit Jeannette, and did on one occasion. I rode past her house hoping she'd see me and perhaps say something the next day at school. It didn't work, or Jeannette wasn't impressed enough that it mattered.

Cricket and I logged several hours hauling grocery supplies and mail together. I think she enjoyed the ride as much as I did.

Ronnie proudly shows off his little mare Cricket, after a few weeks of riding and grooming her.

9

The Harley

Not too long after my tree-hugging incident, Dad brought home an early model Harley Davidson motorcycle he bought on one of his business trips down to Firebaugh. It had big wide tires, broad handlebars, and a very springy seat. It also had a "suicide clutch!" It was called a suicide clutch because you had to push down so hard on the clutch with your left foot it sometimes caused you to drift left and into the on-coming lane of traffic. Matters were compounded by having to pull the gearshift lever, which was also mounted on the left side of the gas tank.

Dad took the motor apart, cleaned everything up and got it running. He painted the tanks and fenders canary yellow and wiped everything clean with a cloth soaked in gasoline. One of the tires had a slow air leak, so Dad put a boot-patch or a heavy patch on the inside of the tire and replaced the old tube with a new one.

After Dad got the Harley going he told me he was going to teach me how to ride it. The bike was so big and so heavy I never thought I'd ever be able to ride it. Dad put me on the motorcycle in front of him and we rode around while he instructed me on the various aspects of riding a two-wheel motor vehicle.

One of the things Dad told me was to refer to the bike as a Harley and not a motorcycle. As a young man, he had owned a Harley and it was not cool to say you rode a motorcycle; you rode a Harley. He scooted back and let me hold the handlebars by myself.

Suddenly Dad stood up and I kept going solo. I was headed for one of the cottonwood trees and trying to turn the Harley. The bike was simply too heavy for my inexperienced lightweight body. I leaned like Dad told me to do and gave it some gas by cranking the throttle counter clockwise with my right hand. I gave it too much gas with the throttle and hit the tree, but not hard. I actually glanced off to the left side trunk portion of the tree and to my surprise didn't crash. The motorcycle stayed right side up, and I was able to slow down enough to ride around slowly for several minutes.

I was given free reign of the many miles of dirt roads on the ranch and spent many hours riding the Harley.

I never had the desire to see what it could do. I had learned that lesson with Cricket in the dry creek bed and felt comfortable with my self-imposed limitations.

The only questionable thing I did was to ride the Harley up a steep hillside one day. I got about two-thirds the way up the hill and my rear tire started to spin out. The bike was so heavy I couldn't hold it up, so over we went. Of course the damn carburetor caught on fire! I really didn't want to throw dirt on it, so I peed on it and put the fire out. I learned this trick when our hay baler caught fire once and Dad peed on it to put it out.

I spent many enjoyable hours riding the Harley and split my time between riding the motorcycle... I mean the Harley, and Cricket. I found I enjoyed both immensely. I woke up bright and early every morning ready to meet the day I knew was going to be different and interesting.

Ronnie had free rein to ride his father's Harley Davidson on the many miles of dirt road on the old Curtner Ranch in Panoche Valley.

10

Darrell

As I rode Cricket into the barnyard late one afternoon, I saw Dad talking to someone I didn't recognize. The two men were in front of the tack room, which faced east and away from the setting sun. Both Dad and the stranger had found places to sit in the shade and were smoking cigarettes. As I approached the men, I saw even though the newcomer was sitting down, he was a big man. I stopped Cricket in front of the hitching post Dad recently made out of three splintery fence posts, and dismounted.

"Darrell, this is my boy, Ronnie," Dad said. "He's been out training his new mare."

"She's a fine looking pony," Darrell said as he stood. "What do you call her?"

"Cricket," I replied. "She's an Appaloosa, but still too young to have spots."

"Your Dad tells me you put shoes on her yourself," Darrell said with a questioning tone of voice.

"Yep," I said giving him a glance. "Just the front ones though; Dad did the back ones."

"I had one just like her when I was younger," laughed Darrell, as he reached out and scratched Cricket's nose. He continued, "Much younger."

"Darrell has a question for you," Dad interjected as he reached out to the hitching rail and pulled himself up from a cottonwood stump he'd been sitting on. "He wants you to help him with something."

"OK," I said. I was puzzled. I couldn't imagine what such a big, tall, and angular man needed of me. He was very tall, probably six four. He wore his clothes like a real cowboy and his predominant feature was a large red mustache. All of this was rounded out when he spoke with a stout baritone voice. His hat looked used and the sweat rings were a testament to this hard-working cowboy. His eyes were warm, honest, and friendly. I knew this was a man whom I could trust. I already liked him as a friend.

"We're going to start running some cattle up the canyon behind the hay fields, and I need someone to check the pump on the windmill up there every couple of days," Darrell said as he pulled off his hat and wiped his brow with a blue paisley handkerchief. "If you're interested, the pay is five dollars a week." He wiped the leather band inside his hat.

"Sure," I said, as I threw the left stirrup over the saddle so I could get to the cinch strap.

"Good then," said Darrell, as he placed his hat back atop his head. "Let's take a ride up in my truck and I'll show you what needs to be done." I stowed my tack and Dad said he'd put Cricket in her stall and feed her for me.

Darrell and I went up the canyon to the old wood framed windmill. I saw someone had installed a new Briggs & Stratton gas engine and attached it to the windmill. Darrell showed me where to put in the gasoline and how to check the oil. He told me he'd leave ten gallons of gas and a quart or so of oil on site for me to have on hand and to use whenever needed. Darrell said if I filled the gas tank and started the engine every two days, a tank of gas would keep enough water available for the cows to drink without running out.

"So it's okay for me to leave after I start the engine?" I questioned.

"Sure, no problem," replied Darrell. "The gas will run out after a few hours, but by then the trough will be filled with enough water to last at least two days, plus the wind will help too. No problem, just be sure to grease the shaft on the windmill once a week."

"I can do that," I answered.

It was just about dark, so we got back into Darrell's truck and headed out for my house.

"Wat'cha gonna do with all your money?" asked Darrell.

"Buy bullets," I replied.

"Bullets?" Darrell questioned.

"Yep," I said, "Dad has a .22 nine shot pistol, and I need bullets to get rabbits."

"Are the rabbits eating your crops?" asked Darrell.

"No," I said, "We eat them."

Darrell just looked and smiled.

I checked the pump and the windmill every two days as regular as clockwork. I kept everything well oiled and greased up. The cows always had enough water, and I was making some spending money for doing something I thoroughly enjoyed. Darrell brought gas and oil up about once a month and gave me a twenty-dollar bill.

The windmill was about a five or six mile ride round trip from my house. I took Dad's nine shot with me nearly everywhere I went on the ranch.

I decided one day to shoot while sitting atop my horse. I took out the pistol and pulled back the hammer. I saw Cricket's ears lay back, but I shot anyway. Cricket lunged so hard I hung in mid air for a second or two before slamming to the ground with a loaded gun in my hand.

When I found Cricket this time the saddle was right side up. Eventually, I shot off Cricket without her even flinching. She seemed to understand something was going to happen shortly after I cocked the gun.

On one occasion after school, I saddled my ride and took off up the hill to gas the pump and grease the windmill. Just past the hay field I rounded a knoll and spotted a coyote. The coyote was attempting to kill a newly born calf that probably had strayed away from its mother. The coyote saw me and took off. I leaned forward in the saddle, kicked Cricket in a run and gave chase. Pulling out the nine-shot, I leveled it just over Cricket's right ear. I shot, but the coyote kept running. I shot three or four more times and the dog-like creature just kept on going. I pulled back on the reins and slowed Cricket to a walk.

About a mile up the canyon just before I got to the windmill, I found the coyote lying dead next to a large pile of rocks. I stopped Cricket who was snorting real loud by this time at the sight of the coyote. She didn't want to walk up any closer to the animal. I got off and led Cricket the last few feet up to pile of rocks and visually examined the coyote. I hit it five times, and was surprised it ran that far after being shot so many times. This was the first animal I'd killed on the ranch I hadn't intended to eat, and I felt a little sad. I piled rocks over the carcass before riding on up to the windmill.

On my way home I spotted the calf that had been attacked by the coyote. It had found its mama and except for a little blood on its nose, appeared to have not sustained any serious injuries. Even though I felt bad about killing the "kyote" I understood I had saved the baby calf from certain death.

~.~.~

The rains came, followed by an onslaught of wild flowers, green grass and new leaves. Newness was everywhere and I felt renewed myself in this mountain setting.

Darrell brought some gas for the Briggs & Stratton, and asked me to accompany him up to the windmill. I climbed into the big white truck and we took off. We drove up to the windmill and dropped off the gas and oil.

On the way back, Darrell gave me thirty dollars and told me the extra ten was for a job well done. He seemed to have a surprise or something for me. I thought it was the extra ten dollars, but then he continued, "You have a few days off for Easter coming up soon, don't you?" asked Darrell.

"Yes, this Friday is my last day in school for the next two weeks," I replied.

"I'm bringing a few cowboys with me next week for the

Spring round-up," Darrell said. "We're going to brand all the new calves and castrate the bulls. Want to help?"

"Golly, yes!" I exclaimed.

"Good then," he replied. "Is ten dollars a day enough?"

"Plenty," I said.

I could hardly keep from choking. Ten dollars a day! That added up to fifty dollars even if I only worked on weekdays! I really didn't know what to say. I was a pretty good rider by now, but I couldn't rope and certainly didn't know how to castrate anything. Surely I must be dreaming!

"Be ready come Monday morning around six, " suggested Darrell, slowing to a stop. "I'll see you then."

"Okay," I said as I got out of Darrell's truck and ran up to the house.

"Mom!" I shouted. "Darrell offered me a job punching cows over Easter vacation!"

"I know, Son," Mom said. "Darrell asked if it was okay with Dad and me the last time he came up the hill. Guess that little mare is going to earn her keep."

Needless to say, I didn't sleep that night. I spent the next few days getting ready for the round up. I soaped my saddle and the rest of my leather gear. I also gave Cricket an extra helping of grain each day. Every time I got the chance, I'd ask Dad a question about what to do on the round up. Dad said things like, "Do what comes natural" or "You'll know when the time comes."

I was up Monday morning and ready to go by 5:30 a.m. I checked two and three times to see if I had everything ready to go. I went out before daylight and saddled Cricket, making sure the saddle blanket was squared off just right. I'd washed the blanket just for this occasion.

Finally, I heard trucks! The sun was just coming up and I saw the light of at least three vehicles coming down the long dirt drive toward our house. The lead truck was Darrell's followed by two other pick-ups pulling horse trailers. Darrell was leaving two ranch horses to ride at our house by this time, so he wasn't pulling a trailer. Then I noticed one of the trucks was Jim's. That meant Jim was bringing his horse Willy. Willy was an old cow pony, but the smoothest riding horse in the county.

The trucks pulled in and I was excited!

"Hey, cowboy," shouted Darrell. "You ready?"

I just nodded in the affirmative, because I couldn't speak, probably because I was forgetting to breathe.

"Been building any fence lately?" a graveled voice came from behind one of the headlights. A silhouette came into view with a hand extended. It was Jim.

"Not much," I said. "It's good to see you."

"You too, kid," replied Jim. "Hear you're our new ranch hand for a few days."

"Yep," I said proudly. "Hope I can stay up with you pros."

Jim laughed and unloaded Willy from the trailer. Two cowboys, one white and the other a Mexican, walked up.

Darrell said, "Ronnie, this is Jake and Jose, they're going to help this week. These guys work with me in the feedlots down in Firebaugh."

Jake was husky in build, but not quite as wide as Jim. Jose was the smallest cowboy, besides me of course. He was wearing a silver belt buckle with a gold colored man riding a bull in the center of the buckle. I liked it.

There were other differences about Jose. His saddle horn was about two times bigger than the saddle horns on all the rest of our saddles. He wore a green ball cap instead of the usual white or manila colored straw cowboy hat. He smiled and I noticed several of his front teeth were trimmed with gold.

"Good to meet you Ronnie," said the two cowboys as they offered their hands in friendship.

"Jose here is a champion bull rider," said Darrell.

"That's the reason for all that gold in his mouth," Jake offered up.

Jose just smiled real big.

I had saddled Cricket long before the cowboys arrived and all the horses in the trailers were wearing their saddles as well. It didn't take Darrell long at all to saddle up while the rest of us checked to make sure the chinches on our rigs were tight.

We all rode off in the direction of the old windmill. After crossing the creek, Darrell wanted everyone to take a pre-planned section of the ranch in groups. I was to partner up with Darrell taking the eastern route to what was referred to as the "back-side" of the ranch.

Darrell and I rode our horses for a couple of hours to the east and then south to the southeastern corner of the ranch where we found three or four cows and a few steers. We took down our ropes and slapped them against our legs as we whistled and yelled, "Up cow." At first the cows were reluctant to go anywhere, but we kept yelling and riding our horses straight at them. Some of the cows were laying down chewing their cud and didn't want to get up from their warm spots on the ground.

Cows are ruminates, which means they have four stomachs. They eat grass and later regurgitate the grass back into their mouths. They re-chew the regurgitated grass and swallow it back to a different stomach. Darrell told me to watch and count the number of times a cow chews her cud and it will be the same number every time. I couldn't wait to test this information.

The cows and their calves eventually began to move down the trail towards the corrals. The dust behind the herd was thick at times, causing us to tie handkerchiefs around our mouths and noses in an attempt to breathe cleaner air. Mom always complained about the smelly condition that came naturally around cows, but the smell of horses and cows never bothered me. However, I didn't like the flies following the herd that kept biting me on the back of my neck as we rode along.

After about three hours, Darrell and I met up with Jim and his partners who had found several cows and calves of their own. We grouped our herds together in the direction of home.

Now we were pushing seventy-five or eighty head toward the corrals. There wasn't much to do except yell once in a while to keep the cattle moving, so Darrell said he was going to show me how to rope.

"Take down your rope and build yourself a loop," explained Darrell.

He demonstrated with his rope, which was made entirely of leather called a "riata." I followed his lead and after a while, I too was roping the heels of the cattle in front of me. I roped the heels; jerked up the slack in the rope, then loosened it, allowing the animal to walk out of the noose. I found this to be tons of fun and it made the time pass more quickly.

Somewhere at the back of this herd, Ronnie and Darrell are practicing their roping skills on the heels of these cattle.

By the time we got back to the corrals and separated the steers that were going to be shipped out from the cows and their calves, it was time to quit for the day. We put the steers into a large holding pen and opened a corral gate leading to an open fenced-in field so the cows could have more room with their babies. Everyone pitched in and threw several bales of hay into the corrals for the cattle to eat. Darrell and I headed out over to the pen holding the steers. Darrell told me to run ahead and get a head count of the steers for him. I took off and had the number of steers in the corral when Darrell got there.

"How many are there?" asked Darrell.

"Thirty-seven," I said.

Darrell looked over at some hay bales stacked near the corral fence and said, "Divide that number by seven and that's how many bales we need to toss in the pen."

I thought for a second and said, "Five, with a remainder of two."

Darrell reached into his back pocket, pulled out a pair of pliers and laid them down on top of one of the bales of alfalfa.

"Take these cutters and cut the wires off five of those bales and I'll fork them over into the pen."

I began to cut the wires as Darrell grabbed a pitchfork that had been left sticking in one of the stacked bales of hay.

Darrell threw the hay over the fence faster than I could cut and fold up the baling wires.

We finished up and rode back to the barn where the pickups were parked.

All that was left to do was to store our tack for the night and feed and water our horses.

As the cowboys drove away into the setting sun, I walked back to the house. My legs and back hurt, but not enough to keep me from having a complete feeling of satisfaction. I'd learned a lot about ranching and was eager for the morning to come, so I could relive this fine day all over again.

That evening at supper, Mom told me she and I were going to go see a dentist in Monterey about fixing my teeth. Apparently Mr. Light called and arranged a meeting with the Crippled Children's Society. The appointment was this coming Thursday.

"What about my job with Darrell?" I fussed.

"I know the timing is rough, but we might get your teeth fixed for free," Mom said.

The next couple of days were pretty much the same as the first day, except I took more water and snacks, because I'd run out of both early on the first day. We rode out in the morning, found cows, and brought them back to the corrals, where we fed them. I opened a gate allowing the cows to go out into a small grass pasture with the rest of the cows we'd already rounded up. The steers stayed locked up in a separate corral because they were going to be shipped out to the feedlot where they'd be fattened up for three months before being slaughtered for their meat.

That Thursday, Mom and I took a bus to Monterey where two dentists checked my teeth. I heard one of them say I had an extra set of permanent teeth, and he was going to qualify me to receive braces. I was happy, but could hardly wait to get back to the round up.

Friday was the last day of the round up and we were going to process the cows and calves on the weekend. Out we rode, just to see if any of the cattle had been missed. We kept the same partners all week except on Thursday when Mom and I went to see the orthodontist; Darrell went with Jose.

"How'd you think that mare would take this hill?" Darrell said, as he looked down a very steep embankment.

"I don't know. Okay, I guess," I replied.

"Let me show you how to do this," said Darrell. "Come on."

We started down the hill as Darrell called out.

"Give 'er her head" meaning to drop the reins, "and sit back on the cantle 'till you get to the bottom."

I had to lean back so hard to stay on I thought I was going to fall off backwards, but I made it. We rode on having not found a single cow so far.

"Here's another grade. Let's lope down this one!" exclaimed Darrell. "Don't worry. Your pony is 'sure footed," which means she is good in the mountains. Just lean back hard and keep your feet and stirrups way out in front, just like riding a bronc."

It wasn't a statement that made me feel real secure!

"Maybe I should watch once!" I said quickly.

"Follow me," Darrell said as he kicked his horse into a gallop.

I followed and down we went. I felt totally out of control and surely looked the fool, but again I made it without falling off.

"You're a natural, kid. You've got guts," Darrell said, wearing a big smile. "That mare of yours is making quite the cow pony."

We met up with the other cowboys and brought back seven head that morning.

"Go home boys and be back here at six in the morning," Darrell told the others as he latched the gate behind the cattle we'd brought in.

Another sleepless night in Panoche Valley for me! Jim told me he was going to teach me how to castrate tomorrow and I felt a bit confused. I didn't know if I was old enough or if I'd be embarrassed or not. I felt anxious and doubted my abilities.

~.~.~

I heard Dad's voice that seemed to be way off in the distance. "Ronnie, it's five o'clock, get up and eat your breakfast."

"Okay. I'm up," I said grabbing at my blanket.

I ate some eggs, toast with jam, and went out to get Cricket ready for the day that lay ahead.

I'd decided I was going to wait, watch, and listen. Right then, the cowboys drove up to where Dad, who was going to help today, had built a fire. Darrell drove up and got out of his truck, holding several branding irons. He walked over and stuck the big ends of each iron in the flames of the fire, then walked back to the fence to get a cup of coffee from a thermos bottle someone had brought with them.

The cowboys, not saying much, soon put down their cups and seemed to know instinctively what task was going to be theirs.

Jake and Jose got on their horses and started roping the heels of the calves and dragged them over to the fire where Jim was waiting. Jim, the strongest of the cowboys in the pen, yanked the rope off the calf and

120

pinned it still under his knees while Darrell branded the calf and stabbed the calf with a syringe of medicines. The calves had to be vaccinated against several diseases such as Sleeping Cow Sickness and Hoof and Mouth Disease. If the calf was a bull, the rope was removed from its hind legs and placed on its front legs. This allowed the cowboy on the ground to hold the back two legs, stretching the calf so the cowboy with free hands could more easily castrate it.

The cowboys switched jobs after lunch. The cowboys processing the cattle on the ground in the morning became the expert ropers in the afternoon. The morning ropers and equally talented cowboys became "top hands" on the ground processing the animals.

While Jim and Darrell were still working on the ground, they called me over.

"This one's yours kid, cut him," said Jim. "I'll hold him for you. You're going to have to do just what I say and do it quickly, because he'll go into shock and die if we leave him down too long. Here, take my knife, but be careful, you can shave with it."

I took Jim's knife and saw my dad coming over to lend support.

"Grab the sack and cut off the tip to about the size of a half dollar," said Jim.

I cringed inside, but didn't show any reluctance as I followed Jim's directions the best I could.

"Good, now reach up inside and grab a testicle, pull it out to where you can see a good bit of the cord."

I did that too!

"This is where it gets tricky," Jim continued. "Take the ball and squeeze it in your left hand and just tap it with the blade of your knife. The knife is razor sharp so be gentle."

I was concentrating and following Jim's instructions to the letter, because I really wanted to do well at this.

"You're doing real good, kid," Jim announced. "Now let's go on." "Did you see that outer membrane pop back over the testicle when you hit it with the knife?"

"Yes," I said, nodding my head as well.

Jim continued, "That membrane will hang down a bit and help stop the bleeding after you cut the cord. Now squeeze the cord between your first finger and thumb. Push up the excess membrane along the cord and mind the knife," which again meant to be careful and not cut myself. "Okay, great, now with the same two fingers, pinch and rub up and down the cord three or four times while pulling out on the ball with your left hand at the same time to stretch the cord taut."

I did, and was realizing that I was going to be able to do this thing that only men seemed to do.

"There, don't cut the cord straight across," Jim said. "Cut it on an angle and scrape and fray the edges if you can while you cut. That will also help the bleeding to stop sooner."

I scraped the cord on an angle until it snapped, and was left holding the ball.

"Do the same thing on the other side and you'll be done," Jim said calmly.

Thinking through each step, I finished up and Jim's smile told me what a terrific job he thought I had done.   Jim slapped on a dab of pink lard like fly ointment to the open wound and let go of the calf.

After many years without seeing each another, Ronnie and Jim meet at Jim's house, barbeque and reminisce about the "good ol' days."

"Think you can handle an iron, Ronnie?" Darrell asked.

"After that, I think so," I replied, with pride in my voice as I took a deep breath.

"Good then, take this iron and slap a brand on that next calf," Darrell said. "The time you hold the hot iron against the animal depends on the season of the year, which often determines the length or thickness of its hair, and how old it is. These are calves, so four or five seconds will be plenty of time. You just don't want to burn into the muscle, because it'll tend to get infected if you do. Go ahead, give it a try."

I did and the burning hair stunk, but I only burned the hide. Dad said that's all that was needed to mark the animal. I could tell my dad was very much enjoying watching me learn about "cowboy stuff" there in the corrals that day.

As the calf walked away, Jim stood up and brushed the hairs off his hands against the sides of his pants and said, "Good job, kid, real good."

There was no way I could have failed that day, because every one of those cowboys wanted to be proud of me and see me succeed.

~.~.~

A few days went by and Darrell drove up to the house. Dad and I were cutting the tail off a Border collie. It was a cross-bread pup that had been given to us earlier that day by a neighbor. Darrell rolled down his window and told us he'd gotten a job on a cattle ranch in Colorado. He told us he was going to miss the gang and he very much appreciated my help.

~.~.~

Not long after that, while visiting with Jim, he told me he'd heard from Darrell. I learned that the ranch Darrell had gone to was also a place where a cigarette commercial was being filmed and that Darrell had become the original cowboy Marlboro Man.

Photo of Ronnie and Darrell taken in 2001; reunited thirty-seven years after they both left Panoche Valley.

11

"Tailor-made"

Of all the stories about the place back home, I enjoyed most the one where my dad rolled a cigarette while sitting on top a running horse. Dad told me you were a true cowboy when you could roll your own smoke while riding a horse in a flat-out run and make it look like a "tailor-made."

It was difficult not to flash back and remember the hard times at the labor camp in Salinas. Usually at the end of a week, I'd be sent out to look for paper so Dad could roll his own cigarettes. He'd use cigarette papers until he ran out, and of course we had absolutely no money to buy any, so I'd go out and find a substitute of some sort.

I almost always went out on these expeditions alone. Peggy seemed to be captivated by whatever book she was reading. Steve could entertain himself for hours at a time sewing an apron from rags he'd found lying around. Sandy liked to help Dad clean the guns and put saddle soap on the little bit of tack we owned.

Most of the time I'd bring back brown grocery bags, preferably the smaller sacks because they were a lighter gauge paper and easier to roll. The best was a lightweight white pastry sack, which made me feel like celebrating when I found one because I liked pleasing my dad. The white was easy to use and looked more like a real cigarette than the cigar-looking brown bag ones.

Having tobacco never seemed to be a problem. If there was a shortage of tobacco, I found Dad's old cigarette butts and took out the bit of tobacco until he had enough to roll his own. Sometimes I rolled them for him.

~.~.~

I took a pack of Dad's cigarette papers and a cloth pouch of Prince Albert smoking tobacco and saddled Cricket. I rode out to the same plowed field where I had first ridden my pony. The reason was the same, so if I fell off, perhaps the softer dirt would cushion my fall. I put the tobacco pouch in my teeth and took out one of the flimsy papers. I laid the paper between my middle and index fingers of my left hand. I kicked Cricket into a run and dropped the reins on her neck. By now she was in top shape and raring to go. Her nose was pointed straight out and she was in a rip snorting flat out run.

I opened the tobacco pouch by holding it with my teeth and pulling it open with my right hand. I attempted to pour the tobacco into the paper, but it proved to be much like spitting into the wind, and not at all a smart move. I don't think any of the tobacco even hit the paper.

I had to change strategies and do it quickly, because my horse would need to stop sometime soon. I licked my right thumb and index finger and grabbed a pinch of tobacco from the pouch. Then I took the semi-wet tobacco and pushed it into the paper while covering it with the bottom half of the paper at the same time. I did this by pushing from underneath the sheet of paper with my left thumb and rolling it up and over the wad of tobacco against my left middle finger. This action naturally caused my index finger to release upward which left my thumb holding pressure on the partially formed cigarette.

As Cricket's mane flapped in the wind, I placed my right middle finger and thumb next to their left counter parts centering them on the paper and squeezed from the middle outwards to each end of the torpedo shaped object. All the while, I was tucking the bottom portion of the paper down against the tobacco while rotating it slightly clockwise. Jolting up and down in the saddle, I continued massaging the tobacco until it had mostly evened out in the paper, which left a bit of the paper's outside edge or the top of the paper sticking up. This exposed part of the paper I licked heavily, and wrapped it on around itself forming a cylinder. This caused the seam to seal and it was holding!

I gave this newborn cigarette a little twist at both ends. I had seen this twisting action before and now sitting in all this wind the reason seemed startlingly clear; it was so the tobacco wouldn't fall out! I exchanged the tobacco pouch with a box of wooden matches from my shirt pocket. Jostling from side to side, I had become extremely anxious, torn between stopping Cricket and finishing the task at hand. Because of the wind and bumpiness of the ride, it took me two tries to light the cigarette. By now, my hands were shaking from the adrenaline rush, realizing that success was only moments away. I didn't smoke, but took a puff off my creation just to finalize the project.

The hand rolled cigarette didn't look much like a "tailor-made" though, but I suspected neither had my dad's.

I pulled Cricket to a walk and noticed the sweat and lather on her neck and shoulders. I was so thankful for her part in my success, I got off and led her all the way home.

12

The Badger

One of the "back home" stories I heard many times was the one about the wildcat or badger in the suitcase trick. I'd heard this story told many times while listening to "self-appointed" narrators during the story-telling sessions in the afternoons or evenings around the camps.

The person telling the story was never the prankster, but rather it was a friend or a friend of a friend. The story invariably included one of the town's men versus a group of individuals from another town, or "the next county over."

Because of their ferociousness, the animals in these stories were most always a bobcat or a badger. Once in a while a house cat was used, but not without first qualifying the bad reputation of the cat. Perhaps this cat had once killed a dog or something else equally as mean. Of course, the person seeing this prank through had recently caught and caged some sort of a ferocious animal, like a badger.

The story tells of a group of strange men who come in from out of town and drive around suspiciously. The local prankster then took the wild animal, and with great effort of course, put it inside a new suitcase. The suitcase was then taken to a street corner and left out for the strangers to see. Who else would take it, because everyone in town knew of the old, "wildcat in the suitcase trick"?

"Sure as clockwork," the storyteller would say, then go on about the suspicious car loaded with the out-of-towners. He'd tell about how the strangers spotted the treasured filled baggage and after circling the block several times, took the suitcase.

Then the narrator, with full body language, went into a detailed description about what happened next.

The suspicious vehicle always drove off slowly for a half block or so, and then brake lights signaled the beginning of a momentous event. The car doors flew open and young men or boys exited from every portal. The fur and hair would be flying everywhere and embarrassing blood curdling screams filled the streets, which naturally were heard by all the town's people.

~.~.~

Badgers were abundant in our hayfields, and because of their large burrows were hazardous to farmers and equipment alike.

The badger is a larger member of the weasel family. It is wide and has a low-to-the-ground profile. It has short stout legs and long sharp claws used to dig out huge burrows where it lives beneath the ground's surface. They are famous for their notoriously bad temper.

Moving sprinkler pipe was one of my many summertime jobs on the ranch. I drove our older John Deere tractor with a trailer attached that we used to haul sprinkler pipe to the "pipe pile" located on the backside of the hayfield. I unloaded the twenty-foot sections of piping tossing them on top of the mounting pile of aluminum tubes. Dad wanted me to check the oil level in a pump next to the pipe pile. The pump pushed a large stream of water out to the sprinklers and ran twenty-four hours a day sometime for several days at a time. While walking over to the pump, I noticed a very large, freshly dug badger's hole.

Curiosity got the best of me and I decided to walk over and investigate my discovery. I squatted down and looked in the cave like opening. I'd nothing to fear; I'd chased many badgers with a shovel before. I'd always intended to make a badger hairbrush, because Dad told me the badger's hair made excellent brushes, but I never did.

Suddenly I saw a blur of brown and black fur, with a snarling gapping mouth containing rows of white needle-like teeth exposed and coming straight at me! Then my body took over, bypassing my brain completely, and I jumped high into the air. There must have been an adrenaline rush of such enormous magnitude that coupled with my lightweight frame, made me look like a startled deer. I was so high in the air, as I looked down I began to hyperventilate and gasp with short quick breaths.

Suspended animation happened, except in this case I was conscious. I had twenty minutes of deliberate thought in a matter of a few seconds. Time nearly stopped for me in mid air. I looked down and saw the spit-slinging mass of raw ripping power intent on one thing. That was to do me in, no matter the cost. I realized I had to come down eventually and factoring in the badger's forward momentum with my length of stay in the air, I was undoubtedly coming down smack in the middle of the saw-like jaws of my intended killer.

What a time to not have Dad's nine shot! I thought about the badger in the camp stories and why folks only put badgers and wildcats in those suitcases. Badgers could rip ten men apart in less than a minute in those stories. Why was the "bad" in badger I thought? This was a fine fix I'd gotten myself in, and now I had to somehow survive.

I began falling while nasty snorting sounds echoed in my ears. My animal instincts took over again. I thought all I had to do was to spread my feet and legs apart, drop down and avoid the rows of razors zeroed in on me. My reasoning power now peaked, I was thinking into the future. I would hit the ground, jump forward across the burrow and mountain of dirt the amazing animal had piled up the night before, and out of the danger zone!

I was ready. Spreading my legs apart I touched down on earth again, but ever so momentarily. I fell forward and pushed off, launching again into uncharted heights. I was keenly aware of the animal's position in relationship to mine. There was only one other animal present having an equally fine-tuned survival sense as me there amid the pile of pipes, and that furry fellow was proving to be an outstanding survivalist.

I began a summersault, mostly to lengthen my distance from my attacker, but saw I needed to reassess my strategy and I needed to do it immediately if not much sooner. This guy was winning and I needed a plan "B" right now! I couldn't stay in the air forever. Gravity was telling me that this time I had to stay and fight.

The badger seemed to know what my next move was going to be before I did. I knew at this point, I really had to rely on my own animal instincts and raise my level of awareness to at least the same level of the badger to survive this mess. This fellow was going to chew me up and that was for certain.

I hung there upside down in mid air and noticed a rock within reach of the predetermined spot where I was going to again touch down. My back wasn't square with the grounds surface and I knew I was going to land hitting on my left shoulder first. I was going to have to grab the rock with my right hand while it was out of sight, and it was going to be a "one time grab" for me.

My left side touched soil and my right hand miraculously found its mark. I had the weapon! I remember noticing the rock was shaped like a tomahawk stone, and I intuitively began maneuvering it with my fingertips to a position that would best serve my purpose. The stone was rounded on top and had a blunted point on the opposite end. I turned the rock in my hand to hold the pointed end down. All this time I was mentally calculating the position of the beast's head.

The badger has the ability to turn inside its skin and could bite me from anywhere I might grab it, so no touching today! I also knew I could pound on it all day and not hurt the creature from hell.

There was only one option open to me, and that was to strike hard in the "kill zone" which was slightly to the rear and between the now flaming red eyes. This area should put me directly over the creature's brain.

I continued with my controlled crash and rolled out to the left. I saw my most worthy opponent had already anticipated my move and was also turning out to his left to intersect me head on. I waved my left hand across and in front of the enraged eyes as a diversionary ploy. It worked! The bristled, brush-like mass of madness moved to the right. A fatal mistake because this enabled me to reach up and cup my right hand with my left, and bring down the stone with such force it even startled me. The rock met its target as if it were a guided missile.

The badger was instantly motionless. I slumped over the limp animal that lay in the dirt at the base of my knees and tried to regain the breath I'd lost somewhere inside the battle. I stared down at the lifeless shape, small in comparison to me, and I was bewildered at the previous, almost dream-like moment in time.

Later, after telling Dad about the incident, he suggested the badger might have had babies in the burrow to cause her to attack with such viciousness.

I'd gained great respect for the badger that day. Though I had not wanted to hurt the beast, there was no other way.

13

The Foreclosure

It was mid summer 1964. I was going to turn fifteen the middle of next month and with my recent success in school, I was looking forward to going to high school in Hollister.

I'd been collecting eggs for Mom. She was baking a cake and needed some eggs. Returning from my errand, I was about half way between the barn and our house that fateful morning when I saw Dad drive up. He'd been down the hill in Firebaugh on some business at the Co-op. My attention was immediately drawn to his face; it had Salinas written all over it. His eyes spoke volumes to me.

My hands trembling, I was mumbling "no, no, no" to myself. I didn't know what had happened, but I knew for sure, we were moving. The first time Dad's face looked like this was when I was nine years old upon receiving word of Dad's brother's death. I had grown to hate that look over the years and was drowning in desperation at the events I knew were to come with no ability on my part to change them.

I ran into the house and heard Dad say the word "foreclosure" to Mom. I didn't know what the word meant, but there wasn't a modicum of a doubt about our moving. This place was history, and you could have bet the homestead on that fact.

~.~.~

Once, I'd rolled myself up in an old rug with my arms pinned against my sides. The rug was wet and heavy. I couldn't move and no one answered my cries for help for well over an hour. I now had the same feelings of helplessness and panic; desperate to be free, to do as I wished, but staring into a universe deaf to my demands, as I'd once done while looking out the end of the smelly, damp, moldy, dirty piece of carpet.

~.~.~

I loved this place, though, and wasn't nearly ready to leave. My heart sank and I thought of my mare. I had been developing roots here. President Kennedy had been shot and I had gone through that with friends. The Beatles were the craze, which somehow linked me to friends and a beginning or at least a starting point to permanency, something I'd always dreamed about. Living through these things was like building a proper foundation for my future. Security like this I had never known and it was not going to be easily regained. This realization stifled me both mentally and physically. I couldn't think straight and I was quite literally having trouble breathing. My body felt like it was chest deep in water and I strained to move forward. The thought of leaving this place was unexpected and something which I wasn't able to cope with. I felt myself welling up inside, so ran back out to the barn to hide out of fear I might start crying.

Where else could one live where food supplies were delivered three times each week with the mail? This could not be happening!

I had just graduated from the eighth grade. I'd gotten the highest score on the Constitution Test and was looking forward to starting high school. In the same instant, I thought about the old man who lived across the street from the school, and how each year he personalized Halloween bags of candy and treats for all the kids who lived in the valley. I thought about the bar owner whose business was the only one in Panoche and how he'd invite the whole valley to watch Bonanza in color every Wednesday night and give all the kids sodas. There was Jeanette, the girl at school I had a crush on, but was too afraid to talk to her. And Cricket. What the hell was happening? I wasn't prepared for this and would have cried if it had been okay for boys to cry.

Photo of the Hughart's; how hard my dad worked those first few years...

Dad spent the next few days looking for work locally, to no avail. We loaded up and went to Grandma's house in Farmersville. We spent three or four days there while Dad went back out to look for work. He sold the Harley for $50.00 in order to have enough money to go out and find a new job. The ranch hands fed our animals for us in our absence. My brother had covered the chickens with a piece of plastic a few weeks earlier, in an attempt to keep them warm. The plastic was wrapped too tightly leaving no air vent and thirty-five chickens met their death. Libby was gone as well. We butchered her shortly after she had her babies and laid on them, crushing them to death. All there was to take care of at the time of the foreclosure was Cricket, our cow dog, Rippie, and a young tailless pup.

When Dad returned, he'd gotten another job on a ranch in Sonol somewhere near the San Francisco Bay area. I was relieved to learn there was enough room to keep our dog Rippie and Cricket. Dad had given the puppy to one of the ranch cowboys on his return trip to pick up some of our stuff.

Dad's getting a job lifted my family's spirits enough to do what had to be done. We rented a one-way, two-horse trailer, put Cricket on one side and loaded the rest of our stuff on the other. We moved to Sonol leaving behind a foundation of a partially spun web of friendships and memories. I was leaving a part of me I liked and that left me sour, weak, and fragile. I felt exposed and didn't know how to fix myself this time. There didn't seem to be a quick fix, like going across the potato field to fill the water bag had helped me a couple of years earlier in Salinas. This time I felt the pain of leaving friends behind and understand the overwhelming loss of the good life I'd tasted for the past eighteen months. I was beginning to realize what my parents had been searching for during our travels and why their thoughts lived so much in the past.

14

The Warden

The little green house we moved into in Sonol was worse than the house in Panoche, so the cleaning started all over again. We poured boiling water on the walls and sprayed for cockroaches. At night, mice ran throughout the house. Several mice at a time ran over me lying there under the kitchen table. I slept with a stick to fend off the rats when I got up to go to the bathroom.

I remember one night of our first week there; my father came into the kitchen and sat down on the floor beside me. He had his .22 caliber rifle and beat-up silver handled flashlight with him. He settled himself against the wall opposite the sink and said, "I'm going to see how many of those damned rats I can get tonight."

I never told Dad I had overheard Mom telling him she was going to leave, because she was afraid the rats were going to hurt us kids.

I rarely told Mom and Dad things that weren't positive, because I was afraid of causing more worry to their already overburdened stressed out lives.

I remember hearing a rat and shining the light on it while Dad took careful aim and shot it. It was strange being so close to a living creature and looking directly into its bright red eyes just before it died. Knowing a living creature was about to die, made me anguish between wanting to stop the event from happening and having knowledge of several reasons why we couldn't cohabitate with vermin.

I had no problem killing for food or protecting livestock, so why did I feel badly about the death of a rat. I saw rats doing nothing more than scrounging around for food, not wanting to hurt anything and at peace in a dark corner of its world. Not too different from me in my world. Was I in the way to the rest of the world as much as rats were an intrusion to our home?

The move from Panoche had devastated me. I felt myself retreating from the manhood I'd developed on the ranch while working with Jim and Darrell back to the lost starving little nine year old boy with his head on his Aunt's lap going to see the doctor.

I had no desire to make friends or to find a job to help out with buying groceries. My retreat was to a place with which I was very familiar. And I knew very well I couldn't stay there for long without starting to shrivel like some insignificant piece of dehydrated fruit. Past experiences told me to reason through my confused state to get back on track and on the road to recovery. I could help myself this time and I knew it. I just needed motivation.

Irvy's words about there being more good days than bad ones, often gave me hope. I couldn't imagine there ever being other folks in my life like the cowboys in Panoche. But because of the brief encounter with these men, I knew in my heart, I'd be able to continue to improve myself if I tried. Even though I hadn't realized it at the time, they'd shown me I was no longer the intrusive rat with nothing more to do than to forage around for food in the dark.

~.~.~

Dad shot three rats before I fell asleep. I don't remember hearing any more shots that night, so I guess three was all he got. My asthma had kicked up in this damp place and perhaps my wheezing kept the rats away while I slept.

~.~.~

This was an interesting side note to my life. Years later a doctor told me the urine from the mice and rats probably caused my asthma, and the noises I made in my sleep, because of the asthma, probably helped to keep the night stalkers away.

The same doctor also told me that I'd broken my right wrist as a child.

~.~.~

September, two weeks before my fifteenth birthday, I started high school in Pleasanton, a city about twelve miles north of Sonol. It took two whole weeks before I was challenged to fight someone. Amador High was the biggest school I'd ever attended, and I felt completely lost. At least I got to keep Cricket and could enjoy riding her after school. I also went hunting after school and at night.

I loved going out at night with a flashlight and a bean shooter to hunt quail. I'd cut a willow branch where it forked and whittled out a slingshot, or "bean flip" as Mom called it. Then I'd take two pieces of inner tubing about a half-inch thick by about six to eight inches long. Finally, after tying one end of each piece of rubber tubing to the top of each fork, and the other to an old leather shoe tongue forming a pouch to hold a stone or some other sort of projectile, I was armed with a lethal weapon.

Steel shot from a ball bearing worked best as ammo for the bean shooter. Rocks that weren't round sometimes caught the wind and curved off to the right or left, dramatically at times, making it very difficult to hit anything.

After dark, I'd walk up the small canyon behind our house to a spot where I knew quail roosted in some grayish colored shrubbery with thorny leaves. I walked up to within five feet of the roosting birds, shine my light on them, and plink them off one at a time using special stones I'd carefully collected from our driveway. The idiot birds cooed at me while I slaughtered them. I only shot three or four of the biggest birds and took them back home for Mom to cook up for dinner. Dad always told me not to be wasteful with game and take only what I could use.

One cool night while hunting quail, I came upon a skunk. It was a polecat, having swirls of white on its back instead of stripes. It was in some tall dried grass next to one of the thorny leafed bushes right in front of me, and blinded by the light from my flashlight, must have thought it was hiding. The hairy black tail of the nighttime creature was curled up over its back and it wasn't moving, lying flat against the ground surface.

For my entire life I'd been told that skunks couldn't spray if their hind legs were up and off the ground. I reached out and cold cocked the skunk over the head with my flashlight, knocking it unconscious. I thought perhaps I'd keep the skunk for a pet and somehow have its sprayer taken out. Just another wrong decision to tack on to my already bulletin board sized list of life's lessons.

I picked up the skunk by the nap of its neck with my left hand and holding the flashlight with my right hand, supported its belly with my right forearm.

The skunk regained consciousness about halfway back to the house. I was about to learn another of life's lessons. Wives tales were probably just that, void of fact and truth. The skunk was relentless, covering me with a green mist that was almost neon looking there in the beam of my light. I dropped my flashlight and my new pet. My eyes burned horrendously for a few minutes. My first instinct was to run for the safety of my house. There I'd find comfort because I knew Dad could help. At least I could turn on the faucet and rinse the poison from my eyes. I thought the spray had blinded me, and I was relieved to see my flashlight still shining. My eyes and nose were watering so heavily I had to lean forward to allow the clear streams of mucus to drain out.

I picked up my light and ran directly into the thorny leaves of the shrub just like the one that had been protecting the quail earlier in the evening. I heard the flapping of wings distinctive to California's State Bird and was surprised that after all the commotion, some quail stay with their roost. I stopped and took off my coat and shirt. I wanted to use my shirt to wipe my off my eyes and face. I couldn't see well enough to undo the buttons on my shirt, so I ripped it off and was worried that Mom would be very upset with me.

The dry cotton cloth quickly absorbed the tears and was soothing to my aching eyes, which by now were slowly returning to normal. I no longer smelled the foul odor, which calmed me enough to walk home.

I don't know how, but word of my adventure somehow preceded my arrival. Mom greeted me at the front door with a bar of soap and a change of clothes. She stood angrily in the porch light and told me to take off the rest of my clothes, bury them in the back yard and scrub up under the hose.

Funny how no one seemed to notice or care that it was dark and forty degrees out. With my bony frame, it didn't take long before my teeth started to chatter. I think that hose bath was colder than the back of Buck's truck riding to the potatoes fields before sunup. It took several days before I could be around people and not have them quickly excuse themselves from my presence.

~.~.~

There were also deer living in the little canyon behind our house. I made a snare trap out of baling wire in an attempt to catch one. I put a wire noose in an area of a fence where I knew deer were crawling under and anchored the noose to one of the nearby fence posts. Several days in a row my snare would be gone, or the wires had been broken. Each day I'd add another wire to the number of strands I'd left the day before.

Finally, one afternoon after school I checked my snare trap and discovered I'd caught a small spike buck. The deer was still warm to the touch. It was a cool October day, so I cut its throat with my pocketknife and let it bleed out. I dragged the deer through the thick brush and Poison Oak down the canyon closer to my house where I thought I'd feel safer. I put the deer on its back and cut its skin on the inside of one of the back legs from the knee joint down to the abdomen. I carefully made an incision cutting the hide from the groin to girth allowing the steaming entrails to fall out onto the ground. I had to be sure not to nick a bowel that might contaminate the meat with harmful bacteria.

I learned the importance of keeping a knife sharp from my experiences with the cowboys in Panoche. Had I been old enough, I could have shaved with my "Old Timer" pocketknife. I'd learned how to field dress or skin an animal, while living in Panoche Valley and had "gutted" my deer post haste.

I had my prize about half-skinned when I heard something behind me. I looked around only to see a Game Warden! I just stood up and tossed my knife on top of the still steaming carcass. My heart sank and I momentarily wanted to cry. I was not at all afraid of being in trouble for illegally killing the deer, but rather I was terrified of loosing the meat. I knew Dad would be proud of me and I didn't want to lose that experience.

I must have been a sight to behold. I was still real skinny, bucked toothed and bloody from head to toe. I had literally been caught "red handed."

The warden asked, "What are you doing, son?" He was an older man and his voice was soft.

"I'm putting meat on the table, sir," I said humbly.

"How old are you?" asked the man with the huge star on his chest.

"Fifteen, sir," I replied.

"How many people in your family?" asked the man with the biggest gun I'd ever seen resting on anyone's hip.

"Seven, sir," I said. "I'm the oldest of five kids."

The warden walked a couple of steps closer and sat down on a half-rotted log. He picked up a stick and began flicking leaves with it.

"You know about hunger don't you?" asked the warden who was now staring at the ground.

"Yes sir," I answered quietly.

The warden stood up slowly and said, "I just got a call, so I can't stick around. Don't kill any more deer without a proper hunting license. Oh yes, there is a hunting season you really ought to familiarize yourself with."

Watching the warden leave, I felt as if I was watching Grace itself walk away. And the warden just simply walked out of my life. I was both relieved not to be going to jail and grateful to have the venison for my family to eat.

Still, I wondered how he had gotten a call, because I couldn't even see his truck, let alone hear the radio. I thought I surely must have been a pathetic sight for the warden to leave like that. I finished skinning the small buck and took it home. There was too much meat to put in our small refrigerator freezer, so we called my uncle Johnny, my mom's older brother, who lived in Tracy with seven kids of his own and split the meat with him.

A few weeks passed and again I was told we were moving. Apparently Dad's boss had offered him a cigar and when Dad reached out, the boss pulled it back and laughed. I guess Dad told the man where to go and where he could put his job. I know Mom was happy to be leaving this rat-infested place. Even though it meant moving again, I was proud of Dad for not letting his boss push him around.

I truly didn't want to move again so soon. School was tolerable, the hunting was pretty good and I got to ride Cricket most any time I wanted. I had to support my father with his decision to move on, as a son I had no choice. This move was particularly hard though. I felt like there'd be no end to the moving; no end to battling the bullies or hunger; no end to leaving friends behind and no end to being too cold or too hot. I wanted to be warm inside with something nice to look forward to. Even though those people who had helped me in the past weren't around, I wanted them to be proud of me. I vowed to take note of things I thought of as mistakes, and go forward working all the while on a plan for a better future. I was realizing that my world and the people in it weren't changing much, but I was. I left Sonol tired, but with a renewed vigor to learn how to make my life better.

We moved to Tracy, a city not very far inland from Sonol, close to my Uncle Johnny, who helped us find a house. The house was cardboard thin and rickety. It looked like it would fall down if a stiff breeze blew by. The yard was dried up and unkempt, not a single blade of grass pushed up through the baked dirt. It had cockroaches marching across the kitchen floor like an army, and I admired their bravery. The floor of the house was cement, and had been painted gray in some areas and a reddish rust color in others—whatever paints the landlord had available, probably. It was the coldest floor I had ever slept on. I wore double socks at night, not only to keep warm in bed, but also to keep my feet from aching while walking to the bathroom. The hardness of the cement made sleeping next to impossible. There was a small three brick gas heater that reminded me of the one in Panoche School. The heater I used to thaw my frozen body in the mornings was located in the living room, and I'll never forget how comfortable the warmth radiating from the chalk like bricks felt after a night on the painted cement floor. Mom and Dad wouldn't let the heater burn during the night; they were afraid that toxic fumes might suffocate us. All and all, the house wasn't as bad as cabin #44 in Salinas, except maybe for the cement floor.

We'd moved before Dad found a new job, so food was scarce. I had noticed a small canal near our house and decided to check it out. As luck would have it, the canal was drying up. This meant if I kept a close watch, I could get the fish before the night animals did.

I enjoyed fishing as much as anything, but didn't have much of an opportunity to go. Even as a child I used to pretend fish.

~.~.~

As youngsters, my siblings and I often made our own toys to play with. I made stilts out of old boards laying around for my brother and sisters, who always got a kick out of walking around taller than everyone else. I made tons of "bean shooters" and bows and arrows from willow branches. I whittled out small propellers and tacked them up somewhere facing into the wind. One of my favorite toys was a slingshot like David used to kill Goliath. They were simple as anything to make, with two pieces of boot string tied to an old shoe tongue like on a bean shooter to hold the projectile. One length of bootlace was tied to the users thumb, the other length held in the same hand. Using centrifugal force by twirling the sling over your head held a rock placed in the shoe tongue. The rock was released by letting go of the bootlace not tied to your hand. With some practice, I was able to sling small stones and plink cans several times in a row without missing.

Dad once took the stuffing from an old mattress, cut out a doll pattern from a piece of cloth and made my sisters some dolls. He took an ink pen and drew on the faces, which simply thrilled Peggy and Sandy and Steve too.

One of the toys I always had was a fishing pole. I'd take a willow branch and attach a length of grocery twine with a safety pin tied on to it like a hook. As a five-year-old, I'd go out after a rain and "pretend fish" in mud puddles. I spent hours and hours cleaning and scraping the bark off a willow branch and rolling up the twine on the end of the pole before placing it carefully in a corner somewhere.

Peggy, Steve, Sandy and Billie Sue are walking around on their homemade stilts. Ronnie is the one missing his head.

One evening I took a toad sack down to the canal and caught over a hundred crawdads and took them home. I boiled a big pot of water and dumped them in. They were succulent and delicious. Several yummy pan fish and frog legs came from the tiny canal before the water left it and dried up.

Even though Dad found a job driving a tractor in the sunflower fields, we didn't have enough money to feed Cricket, so I had to sell her. When the man and his son who bought Cricket loaded her up, I was glad no one had said anything to me. If I had been asked a question, I wouldn't have been able to answer because of the enormous lump in my throat.

I tried to look at the folks and smile, but my cheeks felt as if they weighed fifty pounds apiece, which made it all the more difficult to stay composed. The corners of my lips felt as though they were lifting bricks, and I thought water might squirt from my eyes at any moment. At this point in my life, selling Cricket topped my list of the hardest things I'd gone through. Cricket was the only soil I had left under my feet from Panoche. I felt as though I was being tested somehow, and now had to move on, with only my thoughts of the security that living in Panoche had afforded me.

A letter from Grandma came in the mail. She was forwarding a letter from the Crippled Children Society. After we left Panoche all of our mail went to Grandma's house. We got mail in care of General Delivery from friends and family. Mom didn't want to give out our address for fear that bill collectors would find us. Sometimes Mom wouldn't pay some of our bills and used the bill money to buy food. The bills piled up and got worse until we were sometimes forced to move to avoid collectors.

~.~.~

The letter was advising us to return to Monterey and have braces put on. Turns out we didn't have to go to Monterey. Somehow Mom had things changed to a dentist's office in Visalia, a city about ten miles west of Grandma's house.

A few days later I was wearing braces and a very ugly wire headband. This was great for someone who people seemed to enjoy teasing so much.

Life slowed down for a while. Saturday night hamburgers returned, but it wasn't quite the same. I knew however, it was me that was changing, and I blamed no one for our predicament. For the next couple of years, birthdays were awkward and holidays were painful. There was never enough money. I felt sorry for my sisters, because they couldn't have the trendy things a lot of the other girls had. I went back to being quiet and stayed to myself. I didn't feel like one of the guys and never ever thought a girl might be interested in me.

~.~.~

At the beginning of my junior year there was a girl who liked me. I was turning seventeen soon and trying real hard to focus on the future. She was sixteen, as tall as me and had long, flowing, silky black hair, only to be over shadowed by her shinny black eyes. She had long limbs and neck. She was so beautiful, and for the life of me I don't know why she liked me.

Sarah was her name and her family followed the fruit. When she looked at me, I knew deep down inside she was mine—heart and soul. Of course, I started liking her too much, but didn't know how to show it. We met every day after school in the little camp where we lived, called "Slave Camp." We sat in an abandoned car that didn't have any doors. It rested under a shade tree in a nearby vacant lot. I'd pretend to drive cross-country and Sarah navigated us to the next point of interest. We drove all over the world in that "wheeless" Studebaker. Sarah called it our "Stupidbaker" because she didn't like its pointy noise. We drove clear across the Great Wall of China one windy cool afternoon. Sarah sat close to me that day because she said she was afraid of the foreigners. The time passed so damned quickly when I was with her.

One evening, I saw Sarah and she seemed different somehow. She wanted to hold my hand and didn't want to let go for the whole time we were together. When it was time to go home, Sarah held my face with her hands, stared into my eyes and kissed me right over my headband. My first kiss and I was in seventh heaven. What a difference having Sarah like me made about how I felt about myself. I felt full and had a toasty warmness inside. I'd never looked more forward to the next day, than any other day in my life.

Well, the next day finally came, and I combed my hair using Rose Oil to make it lay down just right. When I got to school I couldn't find Sarah. I'd not gone by her cabin that morning, because she lived on the next block over. I could hardly wait for school to let out, so I could find out why she hadn't been there. I hoped she wasn't too sick. I ran all the way home from school and up to Sarah's cabin.

I couldn't speak. The cabin was empty. Like so many things in life I wasn't ready for this. How could this have happened? Where was she going? Why had I talked so much and listened so little? What fruit was in season and where? I suddenly understood Sarah's actions from the evening before. She had spared me the bad news, giving me one more day to be with her.

"They left last night, Sweetie," a woman's voice came from somewhere. My mind was still racing and I wasn't concentrating on what was happening around me.

Standing in front of Sarah's empty cabin made me feel so ugly and stupid. The ground was wet from recent rains. My shoes had built up large clumps of mud on the sides and heels, which was easy for me to see because of my stupid high-water pants. My hair suddenly felt greased down and it too was stupid. My braces and idiotic headband were stupid and made me look like a cross between a jackass and a bicycle. Why couldn't I have at least had straight teeth?

I turned and ran home. Telling Mom I was sick, I went into the backroom and crawled up underneath a table. I grabbed a quilt from the floor, covered my head and cried myself to sleep.

~.~.~

We moved again after a couple of months. There was another bankruptcy in store for us, other than that, nothing much changed. My grades weren't horrible, but certainly not the greatest. I'd had a taste of success in Panoche. I'd been trying to cultivate a friendship or two and had experienced success in school. Leaving the security of Panoche Valley seemed to have dashed any chances for the stability of building positive memories; the kind you share with friends later in life. Also, traditions for me were some unattainable vapor unable to solidify in three life times.

Life was too temporary and friendships too hurtful.

With the loss of Cricket and then Sarah, the next few months were nothing short of empty for me, kind of sterile and antiseptic, colorless and without much shape or hope. I continued to exist, only able to fantasize of a place where everyone could be happy and proud.

15

The Move North

As a child I heard over and over again, things like, "If we could just get enough money ahead we could get us a place," or "If somehow we could move up north we could surely find us a place." There were many other justifications as to why we didn't have a place of our own.

I was a junior attending Dos Palos High and my father was milking cows for a living. One November day, Dad walked into the house and told my mother that the foreman of the dairy had gotten a job on a dairy in Smith River, California, near the Oregon border.

Dad said, "Ernie's going to work on a dairy up north and wants me to go with him. Want to go?"

Mom said, "I don't know, a move that far is pretty scary."

I was positively beside myself and exclaimed, "Hell, yes, we want to go!" I continued, "Our ship has come in! We will move north, find us a place, my grades will go up, and you know that fishing even at its very worst, is great up north."

Just then Mom said, "Okay."

I learned that Smith River was a small logging community near the ocean about five or six miles south of the Oregon border. Crescent City was about ten miles to the south and was where I'd be going to high school.

One week later we were on the road again.

~.~.~

Just like most all our moves, we arrived in Smith River early in the morning. It was raining and just like so many times before, I was a little disoriented. We had seen a herd of elk in our headlights about an hour before we arrived at out new home. I wondered what elk tasted like and if I could snare one. Seeing the elk excited everyone, because sighting the large deer like animal validated that we'd finally made it "up north."

~.~.~

The new house had floor heaters in every room and every room except the bathroom and kitchen had carpeting! Things were looking up I thought.

We got settled in and I started school. On the first day, I was standing in the lunch line and suddenly there he stood, "The Brute." He didn't have to say a word. I didn't give him a chance to spew his machismo verbiage. I had been here so many times I didn't even care to think about it. I just muttered "shit" to myself and hit him. I punched him as hard as I could right in the pit of his stomach. I also clipped his nose with my elbow to cause his eyes to water, a trick I had learned early on. If he wanted to continue to fight he wouldn't be able to see very well, momentarily giving me the advantage. I heard things in the background like, "The new boy hit him. He must be very brave," or, "For reals, he's crazy." Whoever Brutus was, he must have been the "king" because I never had any trouble for the rest of my stay at Crescent City High.

~.~.~

The high school had a flight program and actually owned its own plane. Since I was a junior starting a little passed mid year, the principal said I had to wait until my senior year to sign up for aeronautics. So I did.

During the summer break I got a job working on a small dairy near Fort Dick, a small community just south of Smith River and surrounded by very tall Coastal Redwood trees.

The summer passed quickly and I signed up for the aeronautics class. I was excited about the possibility of flying a plane. Mr. Wise was the teacher's name, and it was exciting to listen to him. On my orientation flight, Mr. Wise let me have the controls and later, after we had landed, told me I seemed to have a natural feel for flying.

My grades were going back up and there was purpose again in my life. I continued my job milking cows and found the best fishing spots in the slough, which was down the hill between our house and the ocean.

Every morning, Mom got me up at 3:30, fed me and drove me to the dairy in Fort Dick. I gathered and milked fifty cows with another young man named Darrell. After milking, I changed clothes and caught the school bus in front of the barn. After school, I rode the bus back to the dairy, got off, and changed back into my work clothes. Then Darrell and I repeated the process all over again. Mom picked me up between 6:30 and 7:00 and we'd be home in time for dinner. I did this so I could pay for flying lessons, which I was taking on weekends. They were a little expensive at $4.00 an hour. I gave most of my paycheck to Mom and Dad to buy gas and food. My paychecks weren't much at eighty-five cents an hour. I kept only enough money to pay for one or sometime two hours of flight time per week.

I really enjoyed Friday night dinners. After milking, Mom picked me up as usual. Once in a while I'd drive us leisurely back home where I knew it would be warm and dry. We ate dinner as I told everyone where I 'd be flying the next day, and what Mr. Wise said we'd be doing with the airplane.

~.~.~

I soloed after thirteen hours and had my shirt ripped off as is traditional. I went out flying on my own and practiced techniques Mr. Wise had taught me. I flew to Smith River and practiced short and soft field take-offs and landings on a small airstrip within walking distance south of Ship Ashore. A ship had been moved to a dry land dock and turned into a tourist stop. It was located right next to the Highway 101 about one mile north of Smith River, and big enough to make an excellent visual landmark for pilots.

Eighty-foot tall Coastal Redwood trees lined both ends of the pasture runway, making it to say the least, exciting to land and take off from. I had to slip the aircraft in, which means to cross control and point one of the wings toward the ground. This slipping action, hard right rudder and hard left aileron, depending on wind direction and which wing you wanted to point toward the ground, caused the airplane to lose some of its lift and descend more rapidly. This enabled me to land closer to the end of the runway, which gave me more of it to use during landing and I needed all of it!

To take off, I had to pull on twenty percent flaps, or two notches on the flaps bar, and rev up the engine to full power with the brakes on until the plane began to lunge back and forth or "wheelbarrow" in place. Now, I had to hold the nose wheel of the airplane just off the grass to prevent damage as best I could while gaining speed. The moment of truth was when I had to pull up hard near the end of the runway, and hope I had enough speed and headwind to lift me over the trees. After I cleared the trees, I pushed forward hard on the wheel causing the nose of the aircraft to drop quickly, then banked sharply turning out over the ocean. I thought this was loads of fun and landed in Smith River at least once a weekend.

This made school different for me. I'd tell schoolmates of my adventures and they seemed to enjoy listening. Having a group of individuals interested in what I had to say was new and scary for me. Having told a story about one of my flying adventures made me feel like those who had been listening might think the worst of me. I thought they'd think I was bragging or showing off. This in turn made me feel shallow inside and less likely to say something when the opportunity arose. I liked being able to tell my story though, and felt like this was my rite of passage. I was being successful at something not a lot of people could do. This was further proof I wasn't retarded and kind of sealed that notion. I was also encouraged by my father's approval. When he told folks of my flying abilities, I felt the pride in his voice. I liked it when my Daddy was happy.

My most memorable flight experience was one Saturday morning just after leaving Crescent City airport on a solo flight. I was about five miles north of the airport and over the ocean, looking down on a pod of Grey Whales when I received a call from Crescent City Radio. The station, where the Flight Service Station for Crescent City Radio was manned, was also located on the airport.

"Piper, Niner-Eight, One-One Delta, Crescent City Radio" a man's voice announced above the roar of the plane's engine.

"Crescent City Radio, Piper, Niner-Eight, One-One Delta, go ahead," I answered holding the mike close to my lips.

"One-One Delta, be advised the weather is closing, suggest you return A.S.A.P.," came back over the radio.

"Crescent City Radio, One-One Delta, Roger. I'm approximately five miles north requesting airport advisories on one twenty-three point six," I replied. I wouldn't have normally ended with one twenty-three point six, because they had called me and knew what channel I was working on, but the call made me slightly nervous.

"Copy One-One Delta, ceiling twelve hundred feet, winds, two eight zero at fifteen knots, altimeter two niner-niner-six."

I answered, "Roger, One-One Delta."

I headed for the barn as they say, and at about three miles out I was flying at about one thousand feet, so I called it in.

"Crescent City Radio, Niner-Eight One-One Delta."

"One-One Delta, go ahead," answered the same voice as before. "My ceiling is one thousand and dropping," I said with a question mark inflection in my voice.

"Negative," One-One Delta. Your ceiling is twelve hundred feet and holding," said the voice coming from my instrument panel.

"Roger," I replied. I was about one mile out, perhaps a tad more and now flying at six hundred feet AGL, (Above Ground Level), a good six or seven hundred feet below VFR (Visual Flight Rules) minimums. So I called, "Crescent City Radio, One-One Delta, I am showing six hundred feet AGL, I need to start for my alternate airport."

"Negative! Negative!" the voice exclaimed. "Your ceiling is twelve hundred feet and is going to stay twelve hundred feet. You are cleared to land."

Again I said, "Roger." I continued and slipped the plane on a straight in approach to get down faster. All those testy landings at Ship Ashore were paying off.

Just as my wheels touched the runway, it got so foggy I was unable to see the taxiway turn off that was less than two hundred feet in front of me. I could no longer see the radio station nor could the man in the station see me.

I turned off the runway by using the runway lights that had been turned on especially for me and noticed how quiet the radio was, so turning onto the taxiway I said, "Niner-Eight, One-One Delta, down and clear the runway."

A moment of delay, "Nice to have you home, One-One Delta," said the voice in the box on the dashboard.

"Thank you, sir. One-One Delta out." That was my last transmission for the day.

I had logged less than twenty hours of actual flight time when this happened, and I am sure the voice in the box, whoever he was, had saved my life. I would have had to climb out through several hundred feet of dense clouds using only instruments to get higher than the mountains that surrounded the airport. I probably wouldn't have been able to make such a climb through heavy fog given my level of experience.

Thanks to the hero in the box, I went on to log forty-four hours and took a couple of cross-country trips before graduation.

Ronnie standing next to Piper 9811D just after he'd soloed.

In the days leading up to graduation, I thought about college more and more. My folks never encouraged me to go to college. They pretty much thought I'd graduate, get a job and help out the family until I got married. I overheard Dad once telling Mom I'd soon be out of school and could help out more. This distressed me a little, because I was doing well in school and was up for an academic scholarship. College was indeed on my mind.

I had learned to fly, my grades had again improved, and I was talking to girls. Talking to girls was extremely hard because my self-esteem was seriously lacking, and I was still wearing the gnarly stupid looking headgear.

~.~.~

I'd been traveling to Visalia via Grey Hound Bus every three or four months to have my braces tightened. I usually traveled on Thursday, see the orthodontist on Friday, stay at Grandma's in Farmersville through Saturday and go home on a return ticket Sunday.

One Saturday morning I was helping Grandpa clean up his garage. He pulled out a red pack of cigarettes. He usually smoked unfiltered Lucky Strikes or Camels.

"Here, try one of these, they're called Larks and they're new," he said.

The Larks had filters and Grandpa thought they were probably healthier for him to smoke.

"No thanks, I don't smoke," I replied.

"Don't smoke!" Grandpa grieved. "I don't know about the sissies they're making these days."

I stood and stared at Grandpa for a few moments. Normally I wouldn't have stared challengingly or what must have seemed disrespectful to Grandpa, standing erect and squared off at the shoulders, but I was in a state of disbelief at his words. The moments of silence were heavy and lasted long enough to brand a lifetime image of what had just transpired between my grandpa and me.

We went back to our cleaning tasks, but were quiet for several minutes, neither of us speaking. Then Grandpa awkwardly offered to take me fishing and I knew that in his own way, he was trying to say he was sorry.

~.~.~

After nearly four years my braces were due to come off and just in time for graduation. I couldn't have been happier. Just about every day, I overheard other students say things just loud enough for me to hear. I heard things like, "metal mouth" or "It would be too funny if he kissed Martha, (who also wore braces), they'd get stuck together and have to live that way for the rest of their lives" or "Do you see wire head over there?" I had heard many other put-downs over the past three and a half years. I went from being angry and fantasizing about getting even, to feeling sorry for those who teased me, after realizing how really juvenile their actions were.

I'd made a new friend my senior year. His name was Russ. Russ and I became friends after making "Red Trunks" together. The school had a P.E. program where you could attain certain levels or color of P.E. gym shorts. There were white, blue, green, gold, and red trunks, red being the highest or hardest level to attain.

We had to hang from a bar for three and a half minutes, climb a rope from a sitting position and touch the top of the gym in under eight seconds without the use of our legs and many other equally hard feats of strength. I suppose all that hard farm labor paid off for me in the long run, because I passing all of the hardest tests with ease.

One requirement to make red trunks was the "fireman's carry." We had to carry a person of equal size fireman-style, over our shoulders for five laps of the school's track, a total of a mile and a quarter. I carried Russ the required five laps and he in turn carried me.

I still remember that day like it happened yesterday. Being carried on someone's shoulder for a mile and a quarter was the hardest thing physically I'd ever done. I moaned, groaned and complained the whole way. I threatened to jump off several times before the task ended, but Russ refused to let me down. This was the last event before we both got our red trunks, by the second lap I didn't give a hoot if Russ got his red trunks or not, I just wanted off those horrible pointy shoulders.

We eventually crossed the finish line and of course Russ wouldn't let me down until I pounded him a bit. We'd made it and wore our red trunks with pride.

We took driver's training together and Russ went on one of my cross-country flights. Russ accepted me unconditionally. He wasn't embarrassed to walk with me and didn't seem to ever notice my braces or headgear. We hung out a lot, talked about girls, the future and became great friends. Russ was proof that many people, no matter where I moved to, were good, decent, caring folks. I learned a lot from Russ and appreciated him very much.

I had made another friend during my junior year whose name was Jim, who eventually married my sister Peggy. He too was a good friend, something with which I had little experience.

Jim's sister liked me, but I was socially retarded to the point I simply couldn't handle a boyfriend-girlfriend relationship. I was still not over Sarah, and I suppose had put up a shield to protect myself from anymore hurt or sudden and unannounced losses. Until now, I could count all my friends from the past thirteen school years, counting my two--second grades, on one hand.

~.~.~

One clear Friday afternoon I had been out flying. Once in a great while I'd fly after school on Fridays. After I had landed, Mr. Wise was waiting for me at the hanger. He told me to go directly to school and he'd be right there. Mr. Wise also told me he had just found out he was going to be a presenter at that evening's awards assembly. That's when I learned I was to be the recipient of an academic scholarship. Mom and Dad were also there to pick me up, so they drove me to the assembly, but wouldn't go in with me. I guess they didn't feel they were dressed appropriately.

I went inside where Mr. Wise and a small group of parents and businessmen had assembled. Eventually, I was called forward where Mr. Wise said good things about me and gave me two pieces of paper. One was the Scholarship and the other was a Certificate of Merit signed by Congressman Bob Mathias.

I was glad to get the scholarship, because it enabled me to converse with my parents about going to college. Without that scholarship, I most likely wouldn't have gone on to college.

I didn't go to the prom, buy a yearbook or a class ring, but all in all, I felt I had a pretty good senior year.

I got those awful braces off, passed my driving test, registered for the draft, made arrangements to live with my grandparents to go to college in the fall, and graduated high school, all in a two week period of 1968.

After graduation, I got a job driving heavy equipment for the summer on the dairy where my dad worked in Smith River.

~.~.~

In the late afternoons, I trained a Labrador pup I'd been given to raise. I named him Wrongway, because somehow he learned to go to the right when told to go to the left and vise-versa.

When Wrongway was about two months old, my family also was given a baby raccoon that had been orphaned, which we named Tom. I brought milk home from the dairy and gave some to Wrongway and then bottle-fed the baby raccoon. Tom and Wrongway eventually drank the milk together from the same bowl on the kitchen floor and became inseparable friends. They played their days away until one day after about a year, Tom heard the call of the wild, never to return. I think Tom visited some nights, because Wrongway grieved his loss for only about a week, and suddenly was as chipper as ever.

Ronnie's dog Wrongway, and pet raccoon play their days away and become inseparable friends.

I really missed Tom after he disappeared. I remembered how each morning after I got up to go to work, I'd sit down at the dining table and eat a bowl of oatmeal. I'd look across to the opposite edge of the table where two little hairy hands would be reaching up and feeling their way along the plastic red and white gingham tablecloth. I couldn't resist, and delivered a piece of biscuit to the furry hand-like feet. Tom also liked to sit on my shoulders in the evenings while I sat on the davenport and did my homework. Even though I missed Tom terribly, I knew it was right for him to leave

Once in a while I'd walk down to the slough and fish for large perch or Cutthroat trout. One evening I heard rustling in some nearby grass. It was Tom! He'd stroll over and let me pet him before he bounded back into the tall grass lining the slough's banks.

After that chance meeting with Tom, I'd often see him and would take Wrongway to visit with his friend while I fished. If I had enough fish I'd always throw one his way.

16

Olive Green

At summers end, I moved out of my parent's house and into my grandparent's house in Farmersville to ready myself for college. I used some of my scholarship money and some of my own money to buy a car. I attended the College of the Sequoias in Visalia and worked as a box boy in a grocery store about ten miles north in Ivanhoe.

I was going to school on a student deferment and was in constant fear of being drafted into the Army. I didn't want to go to Vietnam and was hoping the conflict would be over before college ended for me. I spent so much time worrying about being drafted my grades dropped below a 2.0 grade point average. I wanted to play, and then go to Vietnam and die, not study my life away and go to Vietnam and die.

Since my life's dream was to fly and to graduate from college, I decided to let one of the branches of service help me with my career goals. I went to several branches of the service and most wanted too much. An example was: the U.S. Navy wanted a six-year commitment to fly, even if I washed out of flight school or so I was told. The U.S. Army recruiter I talked with told me I could fly fixed wing and only have a three-year commitment even if I washed out of the flight program. So I signed up. My timing was impeccable. Three days after I volunteered, I received a draft notice in the mail.

I was inducted into the Army and went to basic training at Fort Polk, Louisiana. After basic training, I was sent to Fort Walter, Texas, and was put into helicopter flight school. I told anyone who'd listen that I was supposed to be in fixed winged school flying airplanes, and I wanted no part of helicopters. I secretly was terrified of helicopters. Too many working parts on helicopters and I wanted the ability to glide if I lost an engine.

No one seemed to care just what I wanted or didn't want. I was so disappointed; I resigned from the flight program. All I ever wanted to do was to pursue a career in flying and I truly was heartbroken to leave flight school.

I heard too many stories of "choppers" going down in Vietnam and killing everyone aboard. I figured I'd go to "Nam" and take my chances on the ground. I had no choice in the matter at this point.

After I resigned I was transferred to the blackbird wing, which was a term for washouts awaiting their orders to ship out. It usually took about a week. While waiting for my orders, I had a chance to talk to one of the instructors from the base. The Warrant Officer told me he thought I'd probably made a smart decision in resigning. He said he'd been sent to Vietnam, but was put in charge of a supply unit that didn't fly. He however, was required to fly some four or five hours a month to keep up his flight status or stay current to fly. He went on to tell me how he took helicopters for check rides after they came in for a routine maintenance check just to stay up on his required hours. The Warrant Office stared away from me as he told his story of being shot down five times in one year and never having left the flight pattern of the heliport. Two days later I went back to Fort Polk, Louisiana, for A.I.T. (Advance Infantry Training).

Upon returning to Fort Polk, everything seemed surreal and not at all in order. I had a three-year commitment from this point on and most likely was going to Vietnam as a grunt, or infantryman, with nothing but a bush between Charlie and me. Charlie was what everyone was calling the enemy.

The first morning there, I was rudely awakened from my bunk. Two drill sergeants, one young, maybe twenty-three, the other older perhaps thirty, were shouting at me. The younger of the two sergeants was an (E-5), and had three chevrons on his sleeve. The other sergeant had two rockers underneath the three chevrons, which made him an (E-7), or Sergeant First Class. It was three-thirty in the morning and I didn't have a clue why they were screaming at me.

"What are you, son?" screamed the older of the two sergeants.

"I'm a soldier, sir!" I yelled back.

"Wrong answer GI, get your candy ass out of that bed and outside of this man's barracks!" the drill sergeant hollered.

"Yes, sir!" I said back with an elevated voice. I hopped down from the top bunk where I had felt so comfortable just two minutes earlier. My feet hurt when they hit the cold barracks floor. I was wearing only olive green boxers and a T-shirt of the same color. I started to put on my olive green pants but the drill sergeant grabbed my pants and jerked them away.

"Is this what you're going to do when Charlie's coming for you? You're dead! Do you hear me? You're dead!" The sergeant was still screaming.

"No, sir! Or I mean yes, sir?" I said, confused.

"Get Outside!" the older sergeant demanded.

The sergeant continued, "Platoon Leader, get these pansy asses outside and put them in formation. And do it yesterday!"

As I ran outside with the younger drill sergeant in hot pursuit, I heard a distant voice say, "Yes, drill sergeant."

The older drill sergeant followed closely behind, shouting the whole while, "Put that private's ass in a front leaning rest!"

Meaning my private ass of course…

"You heard him, soldier, get your ass down in a front leaning rest!" yelled the younger sergeant. I could tell this sergeant wasn't quite as into this game as the older one, because he didn't strain to scream at me like the older one was doing.

A front leaning rest was sort of a push-up position. What you had to do was to cup your hands under your chin and rest on your elbows on the ground while maintaining a push up position. Your body had to be straight and parallel to the floor or whatever surface was under you. It was not at all easy, but a breeze compared to riding on Russ's pointy shoulders back in high school.

The older sergeant, still screaming like a banshee said, "Private, get down in a front leaning rest and do it immediately if not sooner or I'll have your candy ass just for practice."

I dropped into a front leaning rest as the remaining men of the thirty-man platoon fell into formation.

The older drill sergeant lowering his voice slightly said, "Listen up everyone!

His voice was calm, as if he were addressing a group at an ice-cream social or something.

"This here private is leaning for me not because he's stupid, or not because he's going to die in "Nam" or not even because he's afraid to be seen in his "undies." This here private is leaning for me 'cause he called me "sir" and I want this here private to know," as the sergeant started yelling at the top of his voice, "that-I-work-for-a-living… and I ain't no freaking officer!" as the veins popped out in his neck and his voice cracked under the strain.

The sergeant seemed to be losing it. No one said anything, nor did they flinch because of this mad man's actions. The sergeant paced back and forth in front of the platoon of soldiers that were standing under the stars half-naked somewhere in the middle of Louisiana.

"What the hell are you, son?" the half-crazed man yelled as he bent down over me.

I was thinking as fast as I could and grunted proudly because I thought I had figured out the answer. "A soldier, drill sergeant, in this here man's Army!" I shouted as best as I could while holding up the weight of my whole body with my chin.

The drill sergeant stood up and bellowed, "No, no, no! Platoon Sergeant, get these so-called soldiers inside, make those bunks, dress these babies for chow, and get back out here yesterday! When you get back I want to ask this private leaning for me a question."

"Yes, drill sergeant!" a voice shouted. "Fall out."

After what seemed an hour, all four squads of the platoon were back out fully dressed and in formation. As the recruits ran passed I could smell that someone was wearing "splash on" and that made me instantly mad. I couldn't believe someone had taken the time to put on some after-shave while I was outside in the freezing cold and in a freaking front leaning rest! Frost had formed on grass surrounding my elbows. Still I wasn't as cold as I'd been riding to the potato fields in the back of Buck's truck. That kind of cold was different. It was a wet cold in the Salinas Valley and this cold in Louisiana was a dryer cold and tolerable somehow.

The platoon sergeant shouted, "All present and accounted for, drill sergeant!"

The platoon sergeant had been picked because he was prior service, which meant he was coming back into the service for the second time. He wore a snap-on set of sergeant stripes, to signify his temporary status as platoon leader. Squad leaders wore corporal stripes or two chevrons.

The drill sergeant, looking at the platoon leader this time said, "What are you, son?"

"I'm Regular Army, drill sergeant," the platoon leader replied loudly. Regular Army meant the platoon leader was a volunteer and not National Guard nor had he been drafted.

The drill sergeant walked over to me. I was shaking by this time and had broken a sweat even in the chill of the morning. I hurt beyond belief. I felt as I had when I'd taken a beating from the school bully back in grade school. I wasn't going to give this man the satisfaction of seeing me crumble.

"What are you, son?" the sergeant asked.

I struggled with a clinched jaw, "Regular Army drill sergeant."

"Get your sorry ass into those barracks and dress," said the drill maniac.

"And do it yesterday."

I knew by now that "do it yesterday" meant there was no possible way on God's green earth I could move fast enough to make this man, in this here man's Army, happy. I responded, "Yes, drill sergeant, yesterday."

I very nearly could not walk when I got up. I hobbled back into the barracks, got dressed, made up my bunk, and yes, splashed on some after-shave, went back outside and fell into formation.

My attitude sucked at breakfast that morning.

~.~.~

Soon after the front leaning rest episode, while at the shooting range, some poor soldier accidentally shot the range tower. Apparently a trainee was running down the course and tripped. He had failed to lock the safety on his weapon and had been firing full rake, which was what we called full automatic. As the poor slob fell, his

M-16 jungle assault rifle discharged a burst of about six rounds. Although I didn't see it, I was told that one of the bullets from his weapon hit the bottom half of the range tower where all the top brass and visitors were observing.

Everyone, about a hundred-fifty trainee, was put into formation out of sight of civilian visitors, of course. The unlucky "Sad Sack" was told to hold his arms straight out, run in a circle around the formation and repeat over and over, "I'm a super sonic shit bird with fiber glass wings."

I lost count of how many times he ran around us before lunch. The unfortunate fellow was driven away in a Jeep accompanied by two sergeants and a lieutenant. To my knowledge he was never seen by anyone in my company again.

Lunch was most always an olive green box, K-Rations, filled with olive green cans or smaller olive green boxes. Not every box contained the same things though. Two very popular items were fruit cocktail and Marlboro cigarettes. It was hard for me to believe, but every lunch box contained a small box of three cigarettes. Salem's, Lucky Strikes, Cools and Chesterfield, just to name a few different kinds of cigarettes we found in our lunch and dinner boxes.

We were ordered to exercise and trained very hard. Once we even had to force-march the distance of a marathon with full pack and then were given cigarettes to smoke with our meals. I often thought this practice was a bit silly.

The troops, often sitting around and with not much to do, were told to smoke them if they had them.

Unfortunately, I often had them, so I smoked them. I wasn't a fan of fruit cocktail, so I traded for the Marlboros, of course. I thought, "What the hell, I'm going to die in 'Nam' anyway." Besides, Grandpa would have been proud of me.

My attitude slowly but surely eroded. By the time my company went to train on the survival course, I figured it was only a matter of time before I would go to 'Nam' and be killed.

There were a couple of weeks left, and I really didn't care whether or not I passed this course or any other course. Several truckloads of soldiers were trucked out from camp a few miles and dropped off right at sundown. We were supposed to use our compasses or any other technique we had learned over the past several weeks to get past other soldiers acting like Charlie and get back to camp without getting caught. If you got caught, you'd be interrogated and taken back to where you were first dropped off to start all over again.

I got dropped off on a dirt road and heard someone wish me good luck. I went about fifty yards in the opposite direction from camp, which I knew, or at least hoped, would be clear of the enemy. I pulled out my trusty map and oriented myself. I did this by finding the big dipper in the sky as the stars were just coming out. I knew that the two end stars, or pointer stars at the ladle's end pointed to the North Star. All you had to do was to extend the line between the two pointer stars upward five times their own distance and bingo, the North Star. I could have used my compass, but I really didn't want to run the risk of turning on my flashlight and being caught by the enemy.

Knowing the direction of the camp made things easier so I put my map away. Even though there was a canvas over the truck that brought me out, I was fairly certain that I already knew where camp was. The stars confirmed my thoughts about which way to go and I headed out.

My first thought was to stay on what I was now calling the friendly side of the road, opposite Charlie, and follow the dirt road that the trucks were using. I thought this road to be the boundary between enemy and friendly territory. None of the trucks came back by, so I figured they must have gone out to a paved road or perhaps the dirt road continued on around and circled back to camp. My suspicions were right on. I had not traveled two miles and again, bingo! A paved road lay right in front of me for the taking. Just then I saw Ryan, a buddy of mine and I walked over to him.

"Thinking what I'm thinking," I said.

"I think so," Ryan replied.

"I figured we'd hitchhike back to camp. We could just run off into the woods if the enemy comes along and hide until a 'friendly' passes," I suggested.

"Let's go for it," answered Ryan.

It didn't take but a few minutes until a Jeep with a single occupant drove by and stopped.

We ran up to the driver who was a private like us and I said, "Okay if we catch a ride up about ten miles or so?"

"Sure, hop in," said the driver. "You guys part of the exercise out here tonight?"

"Maybe?" I questioned.

"It's okay, I'm cool," the driver laughed out loud.

We went on and soon saw some vehicle lights and a huge bonfire. It was the same camp we'd left less than two hours prior.

"This is good, right here. Let us out here," I said.

The Good Samaritan dropped us off and left. Ryan and I walked up close enough to see well, but not close enough to hear. We crawled up under some bushes and waited for the troops to come in. Ryan and I ate Hershey candy bars, talked about what we were going to do after the service, if there was an after the service for us, and even catnapped some. We smoked a cigarette or two by cupping the lighted end in our gloved hands so no one would see the burning light.

Somewhere in the neighborhood of 3:00 AM, I spotted a couple of trainees walking into camp. Ryan and I simply walked up to the bonfire and waited for the first truck to load and went back to the barracks.

The next day we were given extra hours to sleep. Ryan and I, not needing sleep, went into town, caught up on our shopping and took in the movie, "Woodstock."

~.~.~

I graduated from A.I.T. and received orders for Vietnam, as did everyone except the National Guard trainees. My orders were sending me to Vietnam for sure, but diverted me to Fort Huachuca, Arizona, for special training.

Before I left Fort Polk, the older sergeant that had me in the front leaning rest my first night in camp approached. He seemed strangely calm. His face wasn't contorted as it usually was. He told me he had selected me to lean for him the day before the exercise because I looked to be the strongest in the company and could hold up through the stress of the lesson. He hoped there were no hard feelings and wished me good luck. I couldn't hold a grudge and shook his hand before boarding the bus heading west.

I spent several weeks in Arizona training with a small group of Special Forces. This must have been someone's sick joke for me. I'd resigned from the helicopter flight school, because I didn't want to go to Vietnam in a whirlybird that could easily be brought down with a crossbow. Now my new job not only had me in a helicopter, but sitting out on the skids, dropping radio antenna devices. I was actually sitting out in front of the door gunner whose life expectancy was some four seconds.

Ron standing outside his barracks, where the drill maniac put him in a front leaning rest on his first morning at Fort Polk Louisiana.

I left Fort Huachuca, and went home on a two-week leave. Mom and Dad were living on a dairy just outside Caruthers,

California. They'd moved back down to the San Joaquin Valley closer to Dad's Parents in Farmersville.

My leave passed quickly. It seemed no time at all when Mom and Dad were driving me to the bus station in nearby Fresno. I was headed for the Overseas Replacement Station in Oakland in route to Vietnam. I told Dad not to worry, because I'd be coming back, although I didn't believe it much. Dad had a facial expression I'd not seen before.

Dad wasn't this big, burley, somewhat scary guy anymore. I'd been up against big and burley drill sergeants and some tough Special Forces fellows in hand to hand combat exercises. There wasn't too much I was afraid of these days. I did however, feel an ache in the pit of my stomach when I realized Dad was worried about the possibility of me dying. I couldn't imagine sending my son off to war knowing he might not come home again. I was also saddened I'd not gotten better grades in school and continued to go to school on a student deferment. Perhaps I would have been drafted anyway, but I felt sick at the thought I might have brought such agony to my folks.

For Dad to drive me to the bus station must have been the hardest thing in his life to do. He had no tears and no hugs, just a simple, "Take care." I wish I hadn't looked into his eyes before leaving.

Two days after arriving in Oakland, I'd been issued jungle fatigues and was waiting to get on a plane bound for war. Several hundred troops were called into a huge building; perhaps it was an old blimp hanger or something. Up front on the podium stood a sergeant who was calling out names from a flight manifest. The list was made up of names of troops scheduled to leave for Vietnam on the next flight out. Sure enough my name came up.

"Hugh-gert, Ronald L.," was announced.

I was sitting on top of some folded up bleachers above most everyone else and yelled out, "That's Huggert, you shit head."

You could have heard a pin drop in the building that must have covered more than an acre.

I looked out over the sea of silence and said, "What the hell's he going to do, send me to Vietnam?"

That statement brought down the house with laughter. The sergeant continued on with his list and after about three or four minutes a couple of other sergeants made their way through the crowd and up to me.

"Come with us, soldier," one of the men said.

So I did. I wasn't afraid anymore and it showed. I was a little surprised at my arrogant attitude toward the sergeant. I felt confused, but not afraid. I was ready to go to jail if need be. I had spoken to the sergeant in a flippant manner for the same reason I'd started smoking. I didn't think I'd make it back from Vietnam alive.

The two sergeants, one holding each of my elbows, took me straight to the kitchen where I did several straight hours of KP or Kitchen Police. I had to wash dirty pots and pans, and peel hundreds of pounds of potatoes. My life, growing up the way I did in places like the labor camp in Salinas, was perfect training for the Army. I could fight and peel potatoes with the best of them.

The next day another manifest came down, and this time there were only nine names on it. A battered looking, war-torn Green Beret came forward and called out the names. He too mispronounced my name, but I didn't want to peel potatoes again so soon, so I kept my mouth shut this time. I thought I'd really goofed up with the other sergeant the day before, and wondered what these other fellows had done to be in such trouble. At that moment, I truly thought I'd been volunteered for some Special Forces suicide mission.

After some time the sergeant told the nine of us we'd soon board a plane headed for Germany. He passed out assignment orders that read, "Frankfurt, Germany" on all nine of them. I was in disbelief and truly confused at this point. I thought the Army was out to get me personally. Now this didn't seem to be the case at all. It seemed as if you were standing in the right place and a need should arise, you went.

On the way to Germany the nine of us compared notes. We learned that most of us had two years of college and all could type fifty plus words a minute on a manual typewriter.

All nine of us eventually became Company Clerks in Germany. The Army had called this one right.

~.~.~

It took nearly two weeks to get to Germany. After three days of traveling, I wound up in Fort Dix, New Jersey. I mopped and buffed floors for three more days before getting on a plane headed for Europe. I'd hoped to see the Statue of Liberty while flying out over New York, but a cloud cover prevented that from happening.

My plane landed at the Rhine Maine Airport in Frankfort Germany and before long I was sitting behind a clerks desk at "The Rock" The 3rd Battalion 36th Infantry Division, Charlie Company near Gibsen.

I was to sit at a desk and make up training schedules all day.

Having not gone to Vietnam more than made up for sitting at a desk all day. My typing skills would surely improve and possibly help me find a better job someday. I thought being able to type fifty words a minute was the real reason I didn't go to Vietnam in the first place.

While in Germany, I heard of what was called an Application for Correction of Military Records. This intrigued me, so I looked into the possibility of requesting some time be waived from my original enlistment. What did I have to lose, except my time? I had the time and the position to aid me in such an endeavor.

It took a few months for me to get all the parts of the application together and filled out. Of course it had to be in triplicate, as did most everything in the Army. I finally sent the application resembling a book manuscript off to Washington D.C. and went about my business.

I liked my job assisting in training, and because of it, got to sleep in a smaller room with only five or six other clerks. Everyone else had to sleep in one of the large bay areas with more than thirty other troops.

Part of my job was to fill in the training schedule and to assign ranking personnel to teach certain blocks of training over the upcoming week. When word got out I'd been assigned to make up this schedule, sergeants and even some of the brass, or officers, started treating me like a human being again.

Another part of my duty was to teach classes on CBR (Chemical, Biological and Radiological) Warfare. This was something I'd not thought a formerly retarded boy would ever be doing.

Having this clerk's job enabled me to visit a lot of Germany. This was because I was assigned to a Headquarters Platoon and never had to pull guard duty, which meant I had weekends off!

Seemed as though clerks needed to be in the office everyday and not sleeping after a night standing watch in the cold, guarding the ammo depot. That suited me just fine and afforded me more time for sight seeing.

~.~.~

I remember hitchhiking in Europe was faster than taking the bus. When I needed to get somewhere, I'd simply go out to the road and stick out my thumb. Always, within a couple of minutes a car stopped to help out the "American GI." Often the occupants went miles out of their way to get me to my destination.

Having no speed limit on the Autobahn, which is a freeway in Germany, was sometimes a little nerve racking. Something about traveling in a car at a hundred plus miles an hour and having other cars pass you was unsettling to me.

~.~.~

One three-day weekend, two other fellows and I took a rubber raft and "thumbed" our way up the Maine River. We bought a case of Export Beer, tossed in our mummy sacks and launched our vessel into the unknown. We floated down stream, drank beer and "borrowed" corn from vegetable gardens growing near the water. We stopped at night under bridges and roasted our corn over an open fire while discussing what the future might have in store for us. One evening, we stopped under a bridge in the country and spotted a guesthouse about a hundred yards up the road. As it was dinnertime, we thought it might be good to save our corn, get a steak and perhaps visit with the locals a little. Of course, visiting with the locals really meant to see if there were any girls to flirt with.

The guesthouse was small and quaint, sitting on a hill with a breathtaking view of the river and surrounding hills. It was as if we were standing in the middle of a painter's pallet and the paints were still crisp and fresh. Outside, small cottages with warm, glowing windows, signaling the onset of twilight, dotted the landscape and balanced out the composition of the real life picture, in which we found ourselves traipsing about. There was a soft, sweet smelling breeze that made my skin tingle. The air was so clean simply breathing it made me feel younger like each inhalation was reversing the aging process.

Inside, the lights were dim and a fire flickered from its rock house in the back of the room. There were

194

a few people, mostly couples, all dressed with a freshness that was pleasing to the eye. It was comfortably warm, almost surrealistically so, because of how the thick walls complemented the broad dark wooden beams that held everything tightly together overhead.

The three of us each ordered a schnitzel, a German steak, and dark ale to wash it down. There wasn't much conversation, because I think we all were just a little taken aback by the storybook like beauty of our surroundings.

Walking into the guesthouse earlier, I'd noticed a twelve-string guitar propped against the stone fireplace. Some time passed and I asked if I could play the shinny well-maintained instrument. Not only was I told yes,but it was in a way that made me think the honor was totally theirs. I played a tune or two when three beers were brought over to our table.

"These are, how do you say, on top the house," our waitress said with the friendliest smile ever and complimenting eyes to die for. Suddenly chairs were being scooted up one or two at a time and a small audience soon formed. I played and sang country western songs and the free beer kept on coming.

The evening was most memorable for me. I thought what a wonderful world it'd be if everyone were a little kinder to each other, and shared just a tiny bit more in a manner like the one that had unfolded before me that day. I was reminded of the words in a Beatles song that went, "Life is very short and there's no time for fussing and fighting, my friend." Perhaps it was the "Hansel and Gretel" setting or the beer that made me fantasize about a better world. I thought that night I was on the verge of figuring out how to solve all societal problems. For an instant I felt like I could taste the answers but couldn't quite complete the bite. The answer seemed to lie somewhere between the actions of the folks I had met that evening and my response to them.

After we returned to our little six hundred-year-old bridge and had crawled into our mummy sacks, I fought sleep, not wanting to give up the short measure of time I'd been pivoting in for an evening. I promised myself I'd someday return with whomever I married to experience this little brush stroke of heaven.

~.~.~

We floated the rest of the weekend to nearly the Rhine River, which was now several hundred yards wide, until we feared one of the many huge barges on the river was going to run us over.

As we pulled the raft from the river, I looked up and saw a huge billboard with Darrell's picture on it. I didn't say anything to the other guys about once knowing the man in the Marlboro advertisement, because I wasn't usually believed about once knowing him, not to mention being his friend.

~.~.~

Most everywhere I traveled in Europe people offered to sell me drugs. I smoked hashish, compressed marijuana, on two different occasions while in Germany. The first time, I was going to the movies with a couple of friends and they detoured out into the woods. One of the guys pulled out a pipe and some yellow-colored caked stuff wrapped in aluminum foil. He said this was the best "Choking Blond" he'd ever smoked.

He sat down and pinched off some of the hashish and put it on a tiny piece of cardboard he'd taken from his hip pocket. Then this fellow asked me for a cigarette and took out the tobacco. He mixed the tobacco with the lumpier hashish on top of the cardboard. Afterward he packed a small pipe containing the mixture and lit it. He took a big drag and passed the smoking pipe to me. I really didn't want any, but I went ahead and took a puff. As I inhaled the smoke, it felt like I'd swallowed a puncture vine and I choked, just like the name suggested. Everyone took a couple of drags off the pipe and began telling each other what good shit it was.

We finished up and headed off toward the movies. A short while later we came to a small creek. We had to jump the creek to get back out onto the road leading back to town. I jumped and looked back momentarily. I was astonished by what I saw! I watched the back half of me, slink over the ditch and into my body. I jumped two or three more times and watched myself cross the creek just as I envisioned a slinky toy would.

Out on the road, I suddenly noticed my feet were swelling. Then my calves got really big and I thought I was turning into the caveman cartoon character, Allie Oop. I thought this was great until my thighs got big and then so did my hips and waist. Now I started to worry, because a sudden thought jolted me! What if this "thing" crept to my heart? My heart would surely explode! I became so paranoid I found myself barely able to walk and began hyperventilating. Just as I thought I was going to die, the swelling that, in my mind's eye, was as real as anything began to subside. By the time we reached the movies, I was weak and shaken up a bit, but alive.

I didn't like the drug high so much, but I did enjoy the acceptance of my friends into their little group.

The next time I smoked was in my room and this time the stuff was called "Black Napalm." I took a hit or two just so the guys wouldn't tease me. This was a decision much like the one when I decided to shoot my dad's nine shot pistol off the top of Cricket. Not at all a smart move.

I remember seeing dark brown clouds coming in on me from all directions. As before with the "Choking Blond" a thought came into my head so fast I became dizzy and had to lie down. I again became paranoid and thought if the dark circles of brown fog came together, I would surely quit breathing. When the clouds came close enough and I thought I was in danger, I went over to the third story window, leaned out and breathed heavily. The breathing seemed to work and the clouds floated apart. I repeated this action all night.

The next morning I was talking to my good friends, one of the fellows I'd gone rafting with and told him about my experience the night before. He told me that after I laid down on my bunk, I went to sleep and hadn't moved at all after that. Another friend confirmed this and pointed out I had indeed awakened fully dressed.

I felt stupid and angry with myself, for smoking something I knew absolutely nothing about. I realized there could have been serious long lasting consequences or it even could have been potentially lethal.

~.~.~

The next time I was offered some dope, I said that I'd pass. I was not teased or anything of the sort. When I passed on the smoke, no one seemed to give a care in the slightest. After that, I noticed other guys passing on the pipe when it made its nightly ritualistic circle of the room from one hand to another.

~.~.~

One night I decided I needed a change of pace and went to the NCO Club, which is a bar for non-commissioned officers like sergeants or specialists like me. A friend, Dwayne and I had a relaxing evening watching a floorshow and downing a few rum and cokes. On the way back to our barracks we decided to take a short cut and followed a graveled footpath between rows of three story barracks. A soldier stepped out into the edge of light that dimly announced itself over one of the barracks back entrances. There were two other soldiers silhouetted just in the shadows behind him. Dwayne was a big country boy who liked to drink Jack Daniel's Bourbon and sometimes sang country songs while I played the guitar. Dwayne wasn't well versed in the art of street fighting, this I could tell by the way he positioned himself in relation to the bad guys; I was way ahead of the game on this one.

I knew the olive green silhouette blocking our path was up to no good and he had a knife.

"Who gave you boys permission to walk through my back-yard?" a voice came from the six-foot figure.

"Last time I checked we didn't need permission," Dwayne replied.

"Well, if you want to pass, it's going to cost you five dollars," the self-appointed toll keeper voiced. "Half price tonight 'cause I'm in such a good mood."

"We ain't gotta pay you shit man!" Dwayne insisted.

Dwayne was brave enough, but had had one too many rum and cokes and "J. Daniel's" to be able to back up any physical confrontation. As we said in the Army, his mouth was overloading his ass.

I moved to where I was standing to Dwayne's right and positioned myself in front of the "ass hole" and his silent partners. This so reminded me of the incident with Mr. Hot Stuff and his goon squad back in the sixth grade at Stone Corral School in Seville.

I knew Dwayne was in over his head because the smart thing to do was to turn and go around the front side of the barracks where the well-lighted main road lead straight up to our barracks.

"Come on Dwayne, let's use the road." I interjected.

"Hell no! El Creepo here's not gonna make me pay," Dwayne said, now on the edge of yelling.

"Five dollars or suffer the consequences" said the leader of the lost pack. He continued, "Or, is it you boys wanna take a trip the hospital tonight?" The knife-wielding gatekeeper stepped forward.

I stepped forward and said, "Drop the knife and let's see who's the better man."

I saw that the wannabe bad guy had been drinking, which I thought evened the odds a bit. He fell forward and dropped the knife. I used to practice this move in the labor camps and knew this action was supposed to make me grab for the so-called "dropped" knife. As I fumbled for the blade, the bad guy would then take out a second knife from his back pocket and cut me with it.

This time it was for real, but I was confidant. Compared to the badger I'd fought in Panoche seven years earlier in 1964, this guy was a clumsy oaf, so I played out the scenario. Pretending to go for the "throw-away" knife I saw the other fellows right hand come out from behind his back, just as I thought, I stepped through with my left foot, reached out and grabbed his right fist. I pulled forward and turned out to the left and backed inward toward my opponent crushing his nose with the back of my head and spun back out in the opposite direction. Now, I had a ton of leverage on his now straightened right arm and wrist. I continued to step out and placed my right thumb on the back of his right wrist and squeezed hard while twisting clockwise with all my might. With my left hand I grabbed his arm and pulled down while pushing up with my right hand still twisting. This caused him to have to lean forward, which kept his left arm away from me. A little more pressure and the bad guy went flat on the ground, bloody face first. He had released knife number two, which fell just below my right hand. That was a stroke of luck, but no complaints from me.

By this time Dwayne was yelling, "Kill the sucker! Take his ass out!"

"Shut up Dwayne, pick up the other knife and watch his friends," I said methodically but forcefully between clenched teeth.

I reached out and picked up the knife and said, "Everyone deserves one warning in life and this one is yours. I'm going to let you go and my friend here and I are going home right through the middle of your backyard. If you come at me again, I will take this knife and bleed you out like a slaughtered deer. Nod your head if you understand."

I'd already placed the knife against his jugular and I felt his head move up and down validating his surrender.

I looked up at the silent goon squad who had backed off just like a couple of skinny seventh graders, so I released my grip on Mr. Nasty. The air smelled fowl. I think one of the goons had shit in his pants.

Dwayne and I went back to our barracks without further incident, where Dwayne bragged with excitement to everyone about what he'd witnessed.

I really felt like I needed a vacation, time out, or just a quiet corner with a table to crawl under for a while. I didn't say anything to anyone. I wanted to savior the moment of the new confidence I felt. I had come into my own and could defend myself, defeating all the childhood bullies at once. They had unwittingly given me the skills to become a real man, which to me at the time, I'd just proven.

I really enjoyed taking care of this particular bully and found it well worth the wait.

~.~.~

Another valuable lesson I learned while in the European Theatre, as some called this place was not to gamble. As I sat one evening drinking Black Cat wine and eating schnitzel I'd bought off the base at a local guesthouse, I was asked if I wanted to play some poker. I agreed and played a few hands of Challenge. In this game you were dealt out three cards that you could bet against the pot, which was to challenge any or all other hands at the table. I was dealt what I thought was a very good hand: a ten, a jack and queen of diamonds. I thought I knew what I was doing. Wrong, wrong, wrong, three hundred times wrong!

I bet the pot and everyone challenged me with a better hand of straight flushes to the king or ace. The pot had more than one hundred dollars in it. There were four players in the game, and it cost me well over three hundred dollars to learn that little life's lesson. Some of the players felt sorry for me and gave back a little of the money so I could buy incidentals at the PX, Army Base Store, that month.

I had made enough mistakes lately and was satisfied to eat in the mess hall and catch up on my letter writing home to the States.

~.~.~

I had borrowed a guitar before this, but its owner had rotated home to the States. The next payday I bought a guitar and I sat around at night playing and singing a bit with the guys while sipping on Black Cat wine.

Mom bought a guitar during the time we lived in Panoche and I'd taught myself how to chord songs. I would also have folks show me different things when I had the chance. I'd always had an interest in music.

~.~.~

Once in the fourth grade my teacher took our class over to the band room to try out for beginning band. I was always attracted to the saxophone and when it was my turn to try out, the band teacher wouldn't let me blow on my choice of horns. He looked at me and said, "You're a trombone man. You'd have trouble with the embouchure with those teeth." That was his way of saying, "Sorry, Bucky."

I was happy to pluck the guitar while others sang and had a good time. It was a pleasant way to pass the time away in the evenings.

Ron is sitting on top an armored personnel carrier somewhere in the forest of Germany. He is content to play the guitar while his friends sing country western songs.

One morning during my tenth month in Europe, I received a letter from Washington D.C. I opened it and found a letter advising that my Application for Correction of Military Records had been approved! Then I noticed my release date was less than three weeks away.

The very next day I was called into the Captain's office. He asked that I close the door behind me as I entered the room.

"Specialist, you've been selected for a special detail. I can't, for security reasons, give you the details, you'll find out soon enough." The Captain continued, "You are to report to the head cook in the mess hall at zero three hundred hours tomorrow morning. You'll be given directions then. And soldier, look stract!" Which meant he wanted me to look my very best.

"Yes, sir!" I said with authority.

The next morning, I reported to the mess hall where I found a Top Sergeant, which is a fairly high ranking enlisted man, an (E-8), three chevrons over three rockers encircling a diamond. There were two other specialists like me reporting for the special detail, whatever it was.

The Top looked at me and said, "Grab some chow specialist, so we can get on the road."

"Where are we going, Top?" I questioned.

"Can't tell you soldier, you're on a "need to know" basis and you don't need to know yet," the Top countered.

I spooned up some cooked powdered eggs, took some white toast, a glass of orange juice and ate part of it. There was a covered Deuce and a Half, which is nothing more than a large canvas-covered green truck with ten wheels, parked outside the mess hall. The truck looked just like the one that had dropped me off on the dirt road during survival training back in Louisiana. At least it was the same color.

Everyone loaded into the back of the truck and found a place to sit on one of the green wooden benches inside the covered bed of the truck. The driver pulled down a canvas flap and secured it from the outside. I could hear his footsteps circle to the cab where the Top Sergeant was waiting for him.

We rode for about five hours not knowing where we were going and arrived at our destination at about 9:30 AM. A short time later, an officer approached the three of us specialists. The Captain told us we were going to be servers to a group of dignitaries that were going to meet for lunch. We were instructed to stay out of the way and above all not to dirty our fatigues. Some ninety minutes passed while I watched cooks scurrying around making all kinds of things from shrimp cocktails to fancy desserts. I looked over the countryside and saw nothing but green rolling hills. There were no signs of civilization as far as the eye could see in any direction.

Suddenly, and seemingly out of nowhere, there were six Huey Helicopters in the air and landing near the huge green tent that centered all the hustle and bustle.

The same Captain approached the three of us. He looked directly at me and said, "Specialist, come with me."

We walked over to the rear entrance of the tent and looked inside. I saw a large rectangle made from several tables with chairs lining the outside of each table.

The Captain said, "Soldier, you've been selected to serve General Westmoreland today. Take the food items as they are handed to you and place it in front of the General from his left side. Don't say anything unless you are spoken to. Understood?"

"Yes sir," I answered promptly.

"Come with me," the Captain hurried.

The Captain and I walked up to the entrance and waited until the dozen or so officers and civilians sat down at the dining tables. The two other specialists were being shown what to do by another officer and apparently, were to serve everyone else at the tables.

"Okay, Specialist, come with me," ordered the Captain.

We walked up to the person sitting at the head table.

"Excuse me, General. May I present Specialist Hughart." the Captain said in a clear but low tone. "He will be serving you today, sir."

General Westmoreland stood up, offered his hand and said, "It's good to know you, soldier."

"You too, sir," I replied. And the General sat back down.

I waited at the rear entrance until the Captain brought each course and I took it out and gave it to the General. I repeated this until the meal was over some forty minutes later.

The General and his entourage went out to the waiting helicopters and flew away.

The Top, who had eaten at the General's table, the other specialists, and myself loaded back up and headed back to our respective companies.

On the ride back, I wondered how the Captain had known how to pronounce my name correctly, and why I'd been picked to serve the General over the other thousands of soldiers in Europe. The experience made me feel good about myself. I thought about the teacher who'd said I was retarded and how important it was to know the facts before passing judgment on someone. After all, I had just served one of the most powerful men in the United States Government. Yes indeed, I felt good! I also thought about the wonderful meal I had eaten before we left to go home, which included two delectable shrimp cocktails.

~.~.~

The last couple of weeks passed quickly and it was time to leave Germany. It took several days to process out of the Army, but on February 29, 1972, I was handed my discharge papers. I'd spent a total of nineteen months in this here man's Army.

17

Exceptionality or Disability?

After a few days' travel by air and bus, I found myself knocking on Grandma's back door in Farmersville. I spent a little time living off unemployment and soon got a job working for the Mayflower Packing Company in Exeter, where I thought all the rich people lived. A few weeks of packing oranges changed my mind about the residents of Exeter. I realized I never knew these folks, and the picture of them in my mind's eye, had been painted there by the stereotyping and petty jealousies of others. Then I remembered how I'd felt after serving General Westmoreland lunch, and how it caused me to revisit memories of my second grade teacher. What I'd learned was you shouldn't judge someone without all the facts.

I found that folks in Exeter were pretty much like people anywhere else in the world and I'd been wrong in listening to the blanket statement that Exeter was full of rich snobs. In fact quite the opposite was true. I even thought I might like to live there someday.

My dad's brother, Leonard, whom we called Uncle Pete, was the Principal at Hester School in Farmersville. Uncle Pete wanted me to teach a woodshop class for him, so he invited me for lunch and to see the school.

He had something else in mind. Right away he introduced me to a new teacher he had recently hired. Her name was Ann Dill. She was beautiful and seemed to like me right off the bat. It was meant to be; we were married four months later.

We loved each other and took things in stride. Our wedding day was a day full of everything that goes with getting married. Everything was centered on the bride, and that seemed to be the way it should be. The ceremony and reception were wonderful, with a big family turn out.

Eventually, with the '66 Chevy packed with gifts, we left the party and headed out for Carmel by the Sea. About half way there we realized that because of a breakdown in communications, we were a day early for our hotel reservations. We were both exhausted and decided to stop in the little town of San Juan Bautista, near Hollister. The only motel with a vacancy reminded me of the labor camp in Salinas, which was just over the next hill. It was very late, but at least our "cabin" had an inside shower. The only thing that bothered me slightly was when I turned on the bathroom light and saw roaches. I wanted to boil some water to toss on the walls and run out to buy a can of "Black Flag" bug spray. The room had twin beds, but Ann and I managed to have a good time in spite of that.

July 8, 1972. With the 1966 Chevy loaded with gifts, Ron and Ann leave their wedding reception beginning a lifetime of adventure.

Ann taught school and I went to school on the GI Bill. I attended Fresno State University majoring in education and commuted there from where we lived in Visalia, about fifty miles one way, on Mondays, Wednesdays and Fridays.

For the most part, I enjoyed taking education classes. I did, however, run into one professor who was, to me, a little unsettling in what he had to say.

Mainstreaming was the topic of the day and I thought his lecture was a little off base. He kept referring to specific learning disabilities such as brain injury, dyslexia and developmental aphasia to name a few. One point he made was that exceptional children require special education to realize their fullest human potential. In other words, give children who were behind, special resources to the point they could re-enter the grade level or mainstream appropriate to their age, to give exception, or modify their requirements. Requirements for these children would be based on the level or severity of their disability. He also told the class that similarities and differences of children must be identified in terms of ability to read, think, spell and other imperfect abilities.

I asked if he thought living the life of a migrant child might be considered a learning disability.

"Why would you ask if moving from place to place could possibly inhibit one's ability to learn?" asked the professor grabbing his chin whiskers.

"Well, sir, you mentioned that if a condition exists that keeps a child from learning, that is considered a disability," I said.

"Explain your thoughts to the class," he said.

"Okay," I said. "The word, 'learn' means to get knowledge and the word 'disability' means a disabling condition. This we've learned in class. Seems to me the term 'learning disability' means that there is a condition that exists which prevents one from acquiring knowledge, physical or mental."

"Go on," the professor interjected.

"Then isn't it safe to say if a migrant child is kept from school to pick fruit or to baby sit, that this child's circumstance (a condition which is preventing the acquisition of knowledge) would in fact be a learning disability?"

"Did you read the assignment in your text?" he asked.

"Yes, I did," I replied.

"Then you should know that the term "learning disability" does not include environmental, cultural, or the economically disadvantaged," he suggested.

"That's true, but being migrant doesn't seem to have much impact on children's lives until they enter school," I suggested back.

"Oh!" his voice now louder than before.

"Sure," I continued. "Before that time, their stability is in being with their family members. When a child becomes a student, however, his or her stability also must come from having the same teacher all year, developing friendships, establishing routines, and having a logical sequence in curriculum and circumstance. The migrant school age child wouldn't have this, and this is as physical as many developmental disabilities, giving him or her more problems with which to cope, thus creating the exceptionality. I submit to you that these exceptionalities hold true because they are 'fixable' to a degree."

"How so?" asked the prof.

"Well, that's the identified difference in children, which defines the exceptionality," I repeated.

"All well and good," rushed the professor. "But aren't you speculating and shouldn't you rely on the years of research of those before you?"

"Yeah," I said. "But would the research tell me that the early onset of migrant life be more or less detrimental to a preschool child, than would the disadvantages of inconsistency in his or her education and socialization early on? In other words do researchers study children of migrating parents before they're in school? And is there a significant slowing of the learning processes because there isn't a consistency of education due to the constant moving for place to place.

"Can you provide us with an example of what research might be leaving out?" pushed the professor.

"I think so," I said. "Could the researchers relay to educators that the C's and D's on a report card be the direct results of being a migrant child, because he or she continuously misses twenty-five days of each quarter helping their family survive? They get C's and D's, even though when they have the opportunity to do their work they receive A's and B's because of the existence of an unrecognized exceptionality, which we'll call chronic absenteeism. The rest who are, let's say, average migrant students' and failing or nearly failing because of the lack of study space, lack of time to give to their studies, poor housing and sanitation conditions, or interrupted education that comes with irregular attendance--not to mention, inadequate nutrition. Poor nutrition alone could be the basis for a fairly good argument if pitted against any of the basic psychological processes. I believe some exceptionalities overlap each other. Look, there will always be exceptions. That's my point. Need there be such rigid boundaries?"

The professor his voice lowered significantly, said methodically, "Environmental conditions cannot be considered in terms of a specific learning disability. Your point on exceptionalities is well taken and is certainly worth pursuing, but let's move on."

At that moment, I felt the same as I did when I felt sorry for all the bullies of the world who were afraid to make friends. I realized at that moment that they were the exception and not the rule. I believed most "bullies" wouldn't have become "bullies" with early identification and prevention of identified socially unacceptable traits such as irresponsibility or rudeness. That could have been, as simple as a well-timed spanking or being given a responsibility to perform and ponder, we called them chores in Panoche. I knew that common sense was often left out of the equation and I believed it needed to be an integral part of any successful program.

I didn't feel bad for the professor, because he was a decent, well read man who listened. I felt sad for the system, the part that made the professor stay bound and quoting the text, and how, no matter what, it seemed someone was going to lose out. I knew who that was going to be in most cases. Why change a poor man's history.

I thought it necessary to know that as an individual, I needed to take responsibility for myself and help those closest to me, making the most responsible decisions, based on honesty and without prejudice. I also felt glad I'd been given a special insight and believed I could truly help those persons of different social, economic and diverse backgrounds. I felt as though I'd seen a great deal of both sides of the coin, so to speak.

This helped me realize there were many unanswered questions and the importance of moving forward cautiously. I learned to question the motivation of events and how they affected groups, individuals, and me; a good life's lesson. Irvy had this insight when he said to me, that there would be more of the good days than bad ones, long ago on the steps of our front porch that autumn night in Springville.

18

The First Day of School--Again

I'd decided I was going to become a teacher and not a pilot. I could always learn to fly and I liked the thought of having my summers off.

I had enjoyed teaching in the service, and also learned how much I enjoyed traveling. To become a teacher seemed to fit into my plan very neatly. Ann was already teaching, so why not?

After a year of taking eighteen to twenty-four units a semester, I began substitute teaching for the Visalia School District on Tuesdays and Thursdays.

Another year with Ann's help, a little hard work on my part and the money from the Army's GI Bill, I graduated with a Bachelor's Degree in Child Development. Two semesters of student teaching later, I had a teaching credential and was ready to launch a new career.

~.~.~

I applied for a teaching position at Snowden School in Farmersville. Snowden School had middle and junior high students. I got the job and began teaching mid year 1975. My class was an overflow class, which meant I was going to have kids from different grade levels, to lower overall class sizes. My first teaching assignment was a fifth/sixth, seventh/eighth-grade combination class.

On the first morning at work, I was talking to one of the sixth grade teachers. He told me I'd be going to SCICON with him, because one of the lady teachers was pregnant and wouldn't be able to go.

SCICON is a science and conservation camp located in the foothills above Springville where I had started school in 1955. The teacher told me he really enjoyed taking his sixth graders to camp for a week's stay and hearing stories about Irvy, the old hermit prospector who once lived there. I told the teacher I was looking forward to going.

~.~.~

As I stood by the front door of my classroom, I was reminded of the corral fence in Panoche Valley and the cowboys that worked there. I remembered the teachers in my life, some good and some not so good. I also remembered all the people I'd met and the places to which I'd moved with my family, looking for a place like the one back home in Oklahoma.

The corral fence was a spot where I went to meditate, and for me, a starting point of the understanding of how I was to fit in this race for life. I also tried to teach myself to appreciate the present, without forgetting the past.

It was a quiet corner of my world, there under the shade of an enormous cottonwood tree. There was often a gentle breeze that caused the leaves to speak to me, in a way that brought reams of freshness to my mind.

Symbolic of strength and security, the fence enabled me to sort and compile my innermost thoughts. There, I attempted to honestly separate right from wrong, good from evil, to open my mind to life's subtle differences and still be focused on the truth. I tried to identify myself, to give myself "the place" to be.

With that beginning, I eventually came to the realization of my own understanding of the truth. Years of assembling my thoughts brought me to the understanding that the "place" back home meant happiness with hope. It brought value and purpose to my folks and others like them.

During the Depression and then the war, my parents were scooped up and whisked away like some debris inside a tornado. This happened before they learned to fully appreciate or accept the change. I thought it sad that a half-generation passed before stabilization settled in for them once again.

The cord to those past places was strong and difficult to cut. For those folks, traveling from place to place was really an uncharted road back to their severed roots.

This temporal rift in their lives, without permanency, became an obsession to regain the simpler and less stressful life lost long ago.

I'd been confused about how I should feel without material things or physical things, mistakenly more highly valued by the adults around me, than was emotional security. I learned I didn't have to be afraid to see the positive side of each moment, or what would lie ahead. I didn't have to be fenced inside a forty-acre bubble, separated from outside life experiences to feel good.

Eventually, I saw that climbing over the fence in the direction of change was okay, as long as I went with the notion that I was mentally marking my trail along the way.

My place was a lot like the place back home I'd been told about so much in my youth; it was no more or any less a reality, just a different state of being, and solely owned by me. The truth was, that my "place", my forty acres with a house and a barn near a creek with lots of fish in it, was anywhere I could be happy and feel good about myself.

~.~.~

As an adult, I'd not been left totally void of childhood scars. I found myself putting up huge barriers for self-protection. Protection from what I'd grown to believe true about relationships. I failed to recognize those people who were non-judgmental. I'd spent so much time dealing with bullies and upper-grade girls making fun of me, that I'd become callused. Without realizing the thickness of my shield, I was only able to handle one or two relationships at a time. I'd lost perspective over the years, and had it not been for Ann helping me along, I'm sure it would have taken an equal amount of time to reverse the process and dissolve the hardened protective covering.

My parents settled on a cattle ranch near Woodlake not too far northeast of Farmersville. They seemed to have found an acceptable place to live. Perhaps the Oklahoma umbilical cord had stretched out thin enough over the years to break, releasing its ties allowing my parents to move on with their lives and realize the life on "the place" back home simply didn't exist any longer. They seemed to be happy enough and stayed on the ranch for fifteen years until Dad retired in 1996.

Doris sitting by Dave while he displays his brands about the time Dad retired.

My sisters, Peggy, Sandy and Billie Sue, all married nice guys and started families of their own. My brother Stephen became a nurse, but was the victim of a home invasion robbery/homicide. He died at the age of thirty-four.

The students began filling the room. I followed and walked up to my desk in front of the class. After everyone had taken a seat, I pointed to some words on the blackboard. Turning to my class, I said, "Those words say, Mr. Hughart, that's me. Does everyone know where the bathroom is?"

First year teacher,
Mr. Hughart, 1975.

1
"25" and "25"
(Continued)

Through my daydream like state I heard the backdoor close, looked up and saw Ann walking towards me.

"Hey birthday boy," she said. "Are you coming in or are you going to sit out here in a coma all night?"

"Yes, I'm coming in," I replied as I stood up stretching a bit.

"What have you been thinking about?" Ann questioned.

"Stuff, mainly how much I love you." I said.

"Good answer!" Ann said with a smile as she picked up the fancy plate holding the left over cake.

I grabbed up a bottle of wine I'd received as a present and the bowl of candies. We walked over to the backdoor and I opened it.

"Honey" I said holding the door for her.

"Yes." Ann looked over at me as she entered the house.

Looking at the apple shaped bowl still containing a few chocolates, I said, "How do you suppose those little "M's" are painted on these candies?"